the
lost
shadow

the lost shadow

a novel by
CARMEN FIRAN

translation from Romanian by
ALEXANDRA CARIDES

LIBRARY OF CONGRESS CATALOGING-IN-PUBLICATION DATA

The Lost Shadow
Authored by Carmen Firan
ISBN: 9781737249177
LCCN: 2022932448

ACKNOWLEDGEMENTS

Special thanks to Paul Boboc for the first draft of the translation, for his work and dedication to this book.

The Romanian edition of *The Last Shadow* came out at Polirom Publishers in 2018. (https://www.polirom.ro/web/polirom/carti/-/carte/6594)

A powerful novel, with a theme that's passionate and intriguing at once: the success, as opposed to the failure, of the Eastern European emigrant to New York. *The Lost Shadow* is essentially an intellectual and erotic novel about conscience. Un-adapted, yanked from the context of his origin, Fred is a metaphysician, a reflexive writer who invests himself existentially and ethically in the written word. In a subtle way, Carmen Firan introduces humorous and ironic-satirical accents into the grave and dramatic tonalities of the novel. A must read.

—ADINA DINIȚOIU, in *Observator Cultural*

The Lost Shadow is the dosier of an anxiety. A parable of the circular walls and of the infernal nations, *The Lost Shadow* illustrates the unchanging disease of the immigrant—the sense of an irreversible captivity. Carmen Firan writes the story of an anxious Ulysses, creating an ever more suffocating atmosphere of an inferno, of freedom.

—MARIUS MIHEȚ, in *România Literară*

THE WAITING ROOM HAD NO WINDOWS.
Fred stared at the wall, on which a Monet reproduction
hung somewhat crooked. New York clinics are studded
with impressionists, not because the paintings might
have some useful effect upon the patients, but rather
from a lack of imagination. Yet the impressionists are
soothing. Warm colors. Or pale, like the faces of those
who walk up and down the halls.

Nothing could be heard behind the doors, though
inside an inferno spoke in words, while the machines
measure sadness, fury, fear or the loneliness of those
people whose lives had been turned upside down.
When you can no longer stand it, you sink into earth or
you rise to the sky. Simple defense mechanisms. Some
go down, others up. When you lose your balance, you
feel like everything is spinning out of control. Fred
tilted his head slightly, and then the picture seemed
straight. It depends on how you look at things. True to
the saying: 'Stay crooked and think straight.'

From her booth decorated with red and yellow
charts, a secretary with dark circles under her eyes jan-
gled her bracelets as she talked non-stop on the phone.
She seemed trapped in an inescapable situation, like

the patients who addressed her with lowered voices, each preoccupied with his own passage through the purgatorial waiting room. Only, her own passage through that purgatory had lasted for over ten years since she'd taken up her position as a receptionist, a job from which she'd been unable to either grow or escape. A deep-rooted sadness emanated from her—a sadness of a woman neither young nor old enough to feel comfortable in her own skin, unable to come to terms with her purpose or to wander the world. Just by looking at her might spark the onset of depression. The features of her face flowed resignedly into the collar of a well-worn green shirt such as medical assistants wear in the summer on the subways. Sometimes one sees them with their badge dangling from their necks, to show off the privilege of working in the medical system, one of the few fields that the financial crises hadn't hit so hard. Or perhaps they feel comfortable in their light-cool cloth uniforms. Comfort has become a collective ideal, and it has never been better achieved than in America.

Fred thought about his mother's upright bearing. She wore silk pantyhose even in the summer ("A lady never puts her shoes on bare feet," she used to say). Such grace and eminence! That's how he always remembered her: distinguished, healthy and elegant. Today no one cares any longer about style and how they look; femininity and elegance disappeared with the older generation. Overweight women doze off on the subway with their legs slightly apart, shod in boorish sneakers to better be able to stomp here and there all day long. The death of passion, as Jim, his misogynistic friend, would say.

Still, Jim's words had lost their former acumen. Fred recalled them bored, his thoughts elsewhere. He no longer cared for Jim's once-stimulating exuberance.

"We hasten toward an effeminate age in which the difference between man and woman tends to disappear. And sexual attraction fades, the libido thins out. Men are more and more tired and more and more coy—no more revolutions, idealism, suicides over love, only out of depression. As for these women, I wouldn't be surprised to see them soon cloned, with a chip beneath the ear and wearing shiny overalls, like the Cabal women with icy skin from Star Trek. Some of them beautiful, yes. Frightening and beautiful."

Only that Jim sees things halfway, or just the half that flatters his macho pride. He would go on:

"Actually, in the end we will become an amorphous mass, devoid of individuality, asexual, besieged by the perverse forms of technological development, lined up and numbered by Google, the universal security system. Security not in the sense of protection, but of the world-wide electronic police."

Why recall Jim's statements all of a sudden? What's gotten into him? Just a little more thinking like that and he'd go crazy, confirming Mimi's predictions, or amplifying her hatred toward Jim and his primitive ideas. Primitive, that's what Mimi called them. Jim was a ridiculous failure to her, from whom Fred would do best to stay as far away as possible.

All sorts of noises and beeps sounded inside the four walls, which were painted in a washed-out blue, like a rotten sea. A Latino worker had just gotten around to cleaning the carpet, also nuanced in blue—a calming color? —and the rumbling of the vacuum cleaner was head-splitting. He found refuge by hiding his pain in the pages of *Time* magazine, spread open on a glass table surrounded by burgundy vinyl seats, which lent the waiting room the atmosphere of a hallway filled with mannequins. Fred refused to be one of them, although the claustrophobic space, like a tiny vacation home with a shared bathroom, didn't leave him many avenues of escape.

The authority that you must appeal to nullifies your personality. You find yourself shy and vulnerable, temporarily bound to the other mannequins with which you share not only the waiting room but also the doubts and fears that will be confirmed, amplified or minimized somewhere behind those closed doors. He had lived through this feeling of humility mixed with fear and guilt many times in his life, in all sorts of waiting rooms, awaiting all sorts of verdicts. All of a sudden, you feel that your clothes are rumpled; the expensive brand of your shoes no longer matter; the cologne you used in the morning or the fact that your name was on the front page of the newspaper is meaningless. You wait with others, and this erases your individuality, forces you to become just another of the mannequins—or, to put it differently: *you have a problem*. Otherwise, why would you be here? And those with problems lose their self-confidence. Which betrays us first, the soul or the body? Which can we count on?

His headaches came out of nowhere. All the telephone lines buzzed, call after call. The secretary's voice cried monotonously, falsely polite, intoning the same phrases with a controlled desperation:

"Good day. Doctor's office. How can I help you?"

There must be so many... The fax coming out of the machine rustled like a snake crawling through dry foliage. Sometimes, in a corner, the filtered water dispenser burped. Water was a good idea. His throat had dried out with all the waiting. Or perhaps from anxiety? Authority intimidated him. He was afraid of verdicts. As if he were always guilty. Something that probably came from his childhood, or from the years of living under a dictatorship. Or maybe timidity and fear were just forms of good manners. From respect to fear is a mere hair's breadth. How else could authorities make their mark? What world are we living in? And if we're going to talk about guilt, well, let him who is without sin cast the first stone.

Fred got up, took a paper cup: click, pushed down the flap, and the bubbles exploded as if lava were erupting from a crater. The water jumped madly in the half-empty container, and it seemed as if at any moment the spigot could have expelled a toad into his cup. Naturally, his cup overflowed. With this pressure, they'd be better off using pint glasses.

He had finished signing the papers outlining his symptoms and medical history, put his glasses in their case, stroked his beard, felt for his pipe in his coat-pocket and glanced toward the young woman near him, who was feverishly chewing on a pen. She had probably begun that task a long time ago; otherwise it would not be in a state of such extreme ruin. The plastic was in tatters; only the cap remained, which the girl was sucking on inattentively, as she shook her head, caught between her iPod's wires as if her head were between two electrodes. She glanced toward him for a moment without seeing him as young people glance without registering anything outside of their own realities.

The air conditioning was blowing vertiginously straight at his forehead from an open mouth-like vent above a Monet. Fred was sensitive to drafts; he had to avoid them; that's what his mother had repeated dozens of times in his childhood while pulling his hat over his ears. His American family doctor later told him that *draft* is a notion that belongs, in particular, to Eastern Europe. They both were right. Everything depends on how and where you grow up, on the water you drink and the air you breathe in your childhood. That's the root of it all.

He shifted one seat over next to an elderly woman who smiled generically, lost in her thoughts, with an unopened magazine on her lap. That icy wind aimed straight at his forehead could suddenly bring on a migraine. The terrible headaches were followed by powerful visual images. Sometimes he had the impression that words gushed from his forehead and made luminous circles in the air, like thin white birds; he looked at how they mated gracefully and then set off and disappeared beyond the line of a surmised horizon, somewhere beyond his occipital lobe. The vision left a pleasant sensation, but he remained somewhat annoyed that he was never able to read those circling words, which came in like material forms, fleshy but incoherent. Fred took a notebook with a blue cover out of his pocket—yes, blue was a good color—hastily scribbled something and slipped it back.

He jumped every time the office door buzzed to let patients and medical staff in or out. They passed through with measured steps as the door whimpered slowly to its close. Nurses in all hues dragged their clogs along, technicians pushed strange tables, doctors quickly passed through looking down to face the floor, as if seeing their own shoes for the first time. Madmen's trot. What's he doing here? He shouldn't have given in to Mimi's caprices. His family doctor could have prescribed sleeping pills and some analgesics. What's the big deal? It's true that he couldn't stand that grumpy fat man, who addressed him with a placid slowness, as if he were always just being roused from sleep, with his humid and mollusk-soft hands, barely babbling the words so that your head would start hurting before you understood anything. But Fred would rather have seen *him* for a prescription, had Mimi not been so insistent:

"My dear, listen to me. It's better this way. Do we have a clue where all of this is coming from?"

Curious. She who was a real *know-it-all* giving up when it came to some simple migraines and innocent insomnia. More than half of America is on *Ambien* and pain killers, so why should she be so afraid? He wasn't tired; one might even say that he felt challenged by a suspicious energy, and his head burst with ideas. Perhaps his migraines came from the avalanche of ideas that daily bounced over him, drilling him with questions and slipping him all sorts of strange thoughts? And the insomnia, too?

"Some people can function perfectly well like this. Where does it say that you have to sleep seven hours a night? Waste of time," whispered Fred.

"Yes, dear, but I can no longer stand you reading next to me with the light turned on till 4:00 in the morning and fidgeting non-stop like a fish on dry land."

Dear was the one that angered him the most of all the names she called him. Mimi knew this and used it on purpose. Back then when his words still carried weight for her, he had explained that her favorite, *dear*, was trivializing in its familiarity—or at least that's how it sounded to him—debasing their intimate relationship to a form of locker room camaraderie. By nature,

Mimi was inclined to a kind of triviality, but ever since they met, Fred had promised himself he'd make a distinguished woman out of her.

"*As you wish, love,*" an expression that Mimi had once murmured nobly, restraining herself for quite a while before some years back, changing it to a sharp and irritated "*What are you saying, honey?*" or "*Leave me alone, darling!*" She'd lower her voice into tired tobacco-worn tones, elongating the vowels and muttering the syllables slowly, so he'd get that she couldn't care less, until she got to "*Be serious, dear!*" meaning she no longer gave a rat's ass for what she would've cherished in him years ago. And since she had become Americanized, she alternated *dear* with "*sweetie.*" Another horror.

"I'm going to work tomorrow; what do you care? If only you could get something out of these sleepless nights… You're never going to write that damn book. Or if only I could find something useful in your insomnia, anything…"

Mimi dropped her innuendo-free reign with a soft but condescending voice, pulling the corners of her mouth down and shaking her head like the pendulum of a grandfather's clock about to ring at the top of the hour.

Long ago these words would have stabbed right through his heart and he would have bled for days. Now, shoving the tobacco into his pipe and avoiding her gaze sufficed.

"All right, I'll call tomorrow and make an appointment with that psychiatrist. What did you say his name was?"

"It's on his business card. Rohmer, I think. Lots of people have told me he's a very good doctor. He even treated Nicoleta's husband."

"The one who died?"

"Yes, dear, but it wasn't the doctor's fault he died; a car hit him on the road." Mimi lowered her voice. "When one must die, one dies. You survive cancer and a month later your plane crashes. Let me be."

"If destiny is implacable as you say, then what's the point in seeing Rohmer?"

"There are reasons. Because otherwise you'll drive me nuts. How you live matters too, not just how long you live. You know what I mean… And please tell him everything."

"What exactly?"

"Everything. The history, so to speak."

"What history, Mimi?"

"Your history, dear—not ancient Egypt's!"

"I don't know what you're talking about," muttered Fred as he tried to work the lighter.

"Don't you see that your hand is shaking?"

"My hand isn't shaking. There's no more fluid," smiled Fred—apparently serene—as he pointed toward the transparent plastic lighter in which the liquid moved unevenly.

"Don't be stubborn, Fred. Stop denying the evidence. And then, let's not forget that your mother…"

"What about Mother?" jumped Fred, this time barely keeping his pipe from shaking. "What are you trying to say?"

"Nothing, nothing. Calm down."

"Mother was simply depressed from loneliness. But for you, loneliness is a disease. Same with those doctors. If you're sad, they give you medicine. They've even invented diagnostics for deadly sorrows: a broken heart, have you heard of that? The disease of a broken heart—an emotional heart attack. But perhaps this is what Mother died from, now that I think about it; perhaps Americans aren't as stupid as we think."

"Of course they're not stupid. Stop denigrating this country; the country shouldn't be blamed."

"I'm not denigrating the country."

"Let it be, dear. Why should we even be talking about this? And your mother didn't die from heart break, as you know all too well…"

Mimi rolled her eyes and swallowed the rest of her phrase, as if she could have told him more. But, as always when the talk turned to his mother, she stepped back, feeling how an icy wall sprung between them.

"I know nothing, Mimi. I question myself. I'm besieged by uncertainties and problems. You know it all."

"Fine, fine," Mimi capitulated, bored. "Look, I know this too. If you want, I'll go to that doctor with you tomorrow."

"Don't worry. I'll tell him everything he needs to know. No need to waste your time."

Mimi opened the window wide, and the clanking of the thick curtains, drawn nervously, covered Fred's last words.

"And let's be careful, dear, when we draw these curtains. Look, the curtain rod has come out of the wall and will collapse someday," Mimi said to him carelessly while putting her make-up on before a magnifying mirror, which she placed by the window to have more light.

"We'll all blow up someday, Mimi; we'll swell up, explode and spread through the universe. We'll float in fine particles that the wind will pick up and take by happenstance to the place where our molecules will sprout in other life-forms."

"Really! And what form do you think I'll assume?" Mimi pampered herself for a moment, seduced by the idea of a second life.

"I see you as a duckling."

"What? Are you mad? My dear, if I am to be reincarnated, I want to be reincarnated as myself. Do you understand?"

Fred was roused by the word *mad*, probably spoken unconsciously. But he suddenly smiled cheerfully: he imagined the round, diaphanous atoms in Mimi's hair blown into a silly duckling that would bob up and down on a mountain lake, just like she now tottered in excessively high-heeled shoes through the living room.

"It would be a mistake, Mimi, for you to be reincarnated into yourself. An unnecessary exercise in narcissism. Don't you want to explore existence from other angles? Think about how much you could learn as a duckling. Or a bee."

"Dear, how about putting an end to this nonsense and verbal delirium that don't mean anything to anyone anymore?"

Mimi shook her delicate hands, her nails freshly painted in burgundy, having won new ground.

"Why don't you put this in your books? Or, even better: why don't you hammer that damned curtain rod in the wall?"

"You know I'm not handy with that sort of thing."

"So what are you handy at? Tell me, can you do anything with those hands?"

"Mimi, don't start again. There's not much to be done with hands."

"Oh, sure, sure, it's the head that matters! We know! Eh, dear, everything I've done, I've done with my own hands. And I haven't lost my head, either."

"Nor your legs," smiled Fred, a smile that drove Mimi out of her mind.

She could fight against everything but his smile. Yet, at the end of the day, who did he think he was? Or who could think that he'd still have a trick up his sleeve, that he'd be able to produce something beyond that ironic smile that couldn't intimidate anyone anymore? Or not her, anyway.

"Show your scorn to others from now on, not to me. I carried you on my back," cried Mimi as she showed her real nature, which sometimes rose to the surface uncontrollably and sent chills down Fred's spine even after 20 years of marriage.

He persisted on clumsily defending himself from her hysterics, which were mixed with vulgarity under the pretext of her being misunderstood, wronged, obsessed that no matter what she'd do, Fred would never raise her high enough on his value-scale, where all that mattered were lectures, ideas, metaphysics, silly things that ruin the mind and from which you can't even make money, as Fred had proven with a vengeance.

"Forgive me, it wasn't contempt; on the contrary, I'm purely and simply helpless. Otherwise, I greatly admire whoever… replaces a light bulb, for instance, fixes a pipe or a flat tire."

"Shit!" Mimi interrupted him, knowing that his coy innocent as a lamb's expression was merely histrionics, ironic superiority and the cowardice of hiding himself behind jokes, quotes, cultural references, or playful humility instead of facing her like a man.

She would have jumped for joy at the opportunity of an argument that included shouts and curses. Fred wasn't even able to satisfy that natural need of hers.

"If I disappeared or cracked up, what would you do? Have you thought what it would be like if you had to live by yourself and *manage* on your own—I know how you detest this word: *manage*!—to pay your bills, and everything else?"

"I don't think about this. I see you as an immortal, Mimi, an Olympian, made of marble."

"Shit!" cried Mimi louder as she rolled up her stockings.

Fred stared at her tanned legs—artificially tanned, true, with ultraviolet rays and creams—her legs that had made history. And money. Almost fifty years old now and they were still beautiful, straight and muscular, with ankles like a fine mare's. Perhaps a bit wide in the knees, but her round and hard thighs, two megalithic apples made to defy time, redeemed all.

"One day I will write an ode to your legs," Fred smiled excitedly, staring at her as she raised her skirt in front of him and fastened the hard elastic of her stockings over her silk Victoria's Secret underwear with confident, but jumpy movements.

"Yes, write them an ode," whistled Mimi, having made up her mind to hit him hard. "It's all you've got left, but you'll probably sound lame."

When she displayed humor, even though involuntarily, he almost forgave her aggressiveness. Intelligence and humor turned him on more than a bare breast.

"*Perversity or camouflaged impotence,*" Mimi would have said on one of her good days.

With a fast and unexpected gesture, Fred pulled her over him on the couch. He brushed back her combed hair and proceeded to lick her long neck. He bit her earlobe, lifted her tight skirt over her thighs and made his way between her legendary legs. For a while Mimi abandoned herself to her own surprise, mostly to check his virility—which that morning, curiously, seemed back in shape—and then sprung away from him like a cat outraged by an abusive master's caresses.

"Now? Just as I'm ready to leave you feel like doing it? Can't you see that you're ruining my hair and rumpling my dress?" rattled a flattered Mimi, lending her voice to the indecisive and well-tempered fury that she admirably displayed in moments when she felt desired and important. "And be careful. You're dropping ash on the carpet."

Fred stared at her detachedly, somewhat relaxed, and it seemed to Mimi that the ironic brightness with which he had dominated her all her life had returned to his eyes.

Fred headed toward the receptionist's booth with his papers filled out, and he placed them discreetly on the counter. The livid woman was still glued to her phone, but flipped swiftly through the papers with her trained eye, took one form out and handed it back to him, mutely indicating where he ought to sign.

"Did I forget anything?" asked Fred.

"HIPAA," she answered with a whiny voice, covering the phone's mic into which she had just murmured a new and exasperating, "Hello. Doctor's office... May I help you?"

Fred looked back at her, intrigued.

"HIPAA," repeated the receptionist. "You know, the confidentiality of your information. For the test results to be communicated only to you or also to another person that you need to designate."

"Oops!" Fred longed to joke. "I didn't think of this. What other person?"

"Wife, daughter, mother… I don't know, whoever you want."

"As if it weren't enough that I will find out… why should we trouble all those people that you mentioned? Some of them don't exist anymore, or never did."

"I'm sorry."

"No need to be. If something were wrong with me, which isn't the case, I'd want to protect my wife, not make her an accomplice. Diseases are like crimes, you know. It's good to commit them by yourself. But you can relax, because I'm not sick. And I have nothing to hide. I only came here for some pills…"

He signed under her increasingly frowned eyes and handed back her papers.

The woman stared briefly at him with an indulgent air, somewhere between professional mercy and careless irony. Still talking on the telephone, she placed all of his forms in a yellow chart, wrote his name from the top down on the right edge, and pressed a button on the computer whose screen had frozen mid-way through a game of Solitaire.

Before getting back to his seat, Fred passed by the Monet and discreetly straightened it as he walked by. He couldn't stand paintings that hung crooked. It seemed to him that the entire room went downstream, pulling his head along. An oblique world with tilted poles, forced off-center from too much evil or too much God: he had written about this sometime ago.

The door that led to the corridor with the medical offices had opened with a shrill beep and a nurse tottered in, called out his name and invited him inside. He followed her broad ass down the narrow hall and made way for the young woman that sucked somewhat more briskly on a new pen, her headphones still in her ears. Done! She had escaped, gotten out, taken her prescription and gone off to join the crowd of youths with personality disorders.

From this point of view, he was lucky. In his youth, he had only fought with censorship in an Eastern European Communist country where he had also tasted a bit of glory. Three books, three awards. It's true that this was in a tiny closed-off country that no one cared about, without the chance he'd ever be translated or recognized internationally, but he'd been still young then and national glory flattered him enough. He received elegiac reviews, a faithful public—a golden future that he wouldn't get to grasp there.

In those days he was everything but alienated. He ate not pens but books, and he set his teeth into the rhinos of the regime, who finally gave up either knowingly or through some conspiracy of the stars. And thanks to the same conspiracy, he left for a conference organized by a European cultural foundation in Paris and never returned. There, Mimi came into his life, luminous, fragile, restless. A Romanian woman from the ballet-group of the Fantasio Theater in Constanța, who dreamt of winding up in America and who, till then, had made crepes in Paris by day and danced her nights away in a second-rate theater. She had passed through the border illegally in the trunk of a kind Frenchman whom she'd met by the seaside in Romania. They had had an adventure: seductive and practical. Somehow Mimi convinced him to bring her out of the country, coiled around the spare tire in the trunk of his car.

Fred hadn't been eager to emigrate, even though life in Romania had deteriorated dramatically in the last years before the fall of communism. He'd lived with his mother in a downtown neighborhood with beautiful houses, he had friends and an editorial position at Animafilm Studio, where he was paid little but left alone. He'd discovered how to survive; he was happy he could write and fought tenaciously for the publication of his books—a nerve-wracking process, but part of the game, with all its tricks and bluffs, whose rules he had learned. As inflexible as he was on the political order and as stubborn in uncompromising resistance in an absurd space, he wasn't the adventurous type to leave that world behind. Until one day when things took an unexpected turn and the snowball began rolling and couldn't be stopped anymore.

The doctor, who was much younger than he'd expected, met him in front of his imposing desk, shook his hand, and in a dash fell into his ergonomic chair, which puffed briefly but welcomingly. Fred sat down prudently, inclining his body slightly, as if he were on the go. The doctor, Mark Rohmer (he had glanced at the large-framed diplomas), had bristly hair and a hawk-like look.

On the wall on the right hung the drawing of a human brain opened like a carnivorous flower with blue and red petals. Fred felt his Adam's apple rising and falling in his throat, which seemed to have narrowed. Timid, sensitive, like his mother, ever since his early childhood, his throat contracted when he got emotional.

The doctor went through his papers quickly, while Fred felt like a criminal who ineffectually tries to hide his crime. But he had nothing to be afraid of; he had checked off all the questions with *"No,"* *"Sometimes,"* and *"Other,"* bored by the banality of the inquiries, but happy to observe how healthy he was—no major illness, no surgeries in the past, nothing.

While the doctor looked like he was reading, Fred kept an eye on him, spying on his reactions. But Mark Rohmer had none. He closed his file and opened a notebook, where Fred caught sight of some doodles and bits of drawings, which relaxed him. He even felt sympathy for the doctor, who may, somehow, be like him, his mind wandering one way, while talking about something else.

"Is everything all right?" asked Fred, motioning with his head toward the yellow chart that had been put aside.

"First time with us?" the doctor returned his question.

How silly. What "*us*"? If he'd been there before, wouldn't the doctor have recognized him? Was it a kind of arrogance, disinterest, professional amnesia? Or maybe "*with us*" meant something else; he didn't want to think what. Rohmer didn't wait for his answer.

"Who referred you to me?"

It was already better; he had given up on the *us*.

"No one... I mean Mimi," said Fred, gulping air.

He darted his eyes around the room to stop the wave of emotions that had again welled up out of the blue. The office was tastefully furnished with a welcoming atmosphere, a comfortable couch, small sculptures, live indoor plants, Rohmer's photograph with a tennis racquet and a roguish hat. There was even a pipe on the shelf. Fred glanced at it. The doctor was human too, certainly; he too had moments of loneliness and sin, feelings, a blonde wife, as she appeared in the framed picture on the desk. Who knows, perhaps even insomnia.

"Mother?"

"I'm sorry? Emilia. Her name is Emilia. Why?"

"You said that she sent you to me?"

"Oh, no," smiled Fred, and he felt that the misunderstanding had already given him a leg up over the doctor. "Not mama. Mimi," he whispered clearly. "Mi-mi, my wife. She heard about you from a co-worker and... I'm sorry; perhaps I shouldn't have taken your time. This is only concerning some simple sleeping pills; the family doctor could have prescribed them, but Mimi insisted.

In the end, what I want to say is that I don't have any problems. I don't need therapy or anything else. I need the magic pill, the pill for all ills."

"A pill for all ills? Who told you that such a thing exists?"

Where did all this blabber come from? So many words uttered all of a sudden? With Rohmer's kind, the less you speak the better. What's more, Fred wasn't the type to communicate with strangers willingly. He was horrified by the idea that people come, stretch themselves on that comfortable couch and turn the on the water works, relating their intimacies, dreams, humiliating moments, opening the dark doors of childhood and the protective draperies of the subconscious, revealing their failures. He looked again at the couch; this time around, it seemed to be an electric chair camouflaged beneath brown leather. The doctor caught his glance.

"To make things clear: I'm not a therapist. The couch you see is just an element of design," said Rohmer coldly, somewhat offended by the confusion.

He might not be a therapist, but he's definitely a fortune-teller, thought Fred anxiously, feeling more and more unsure of his own thoughts. Could the thoughts betray him, even them? How else would the doctor know what was in his head?

"As opposed to a therapist, I can write prescriptions," continued Rohmer with vague pride. "I don't think the pill for all ills will ever appear. On the other hand, there are many palliative pills that help a significant number of patients. But let's get back..."

But Fred's mind took off thinking that the name Mimi caused all sorts of confusion. What's more, it sounded like a nickname. The doctor misunderstood that he called his mother, whose name was Emilia, Mimi. Another confusion that he couldn't have surmised except by happenstance. Some people stick to their childhood nicknames all their lives. Mimi's case was different. Her actual name was Miriam, a beautiful name that Fred had struggled to give back to her, but her family's resistance won over. All of them called her Mimi, family and friends alike; her mother had pampered her with that name since childhood.

Nicknames were very common in Romania, both first names and proper nouns. Titi, Gigi, Tanța, Nelu, Nae—in the end, no one remembered his or her own full or real name. And the abundance of soupie, cheesie, kissie, country-ie, birdie, cowie, housie, which gave folks the impression of familiarity in speech. Over here it's simpler: everything is *great.*

"You're saying you suffer from insomnia?" asked the doctor, sketching the tail of a peacock with geometric forms in his notebook.

"The word *'suffer'* seems exaggerated to me."

Fred stroked his beard some more to stop the tremor in his hand. Rohmer stared at him, interested for the first time.

"Would you like to replace it with another word?"

"A temporary discomfort. Or maybe an alert state of being. A sort of triumph of lucidity over wakefulness. Yes, that seems a better fit. And, in fact, in my case it's not unusual. The mind never rests."

"Do you have a healthy appetite?" Rohmer went on in a monotonous voice, ignoring the information that Fred had struggled to squeeze out.

Fred stared at him wryly. It was obvious that he was simply checking boxes. In one of his novels, he had written a scene with a psychiatrist who walked his patient through the standard questionnaire only to trap him in an already-drawn box.

"Why should I not?" A bit of his self-confidence returned to him.

"Dizziness? Headaches?"

"Headaches, yes. But who doesn't have them?"

"How often?"

"More often, lately."

"Lately meaning since when?"

"Two to three months."

"Does your entire head hurt or just a side?"

"I don't have such a big head; I think all of it hurts at once. But I really haven't thought about this. It's an interesting nuance. Do you mean which side, left or right, the feminine or the masculine?"

"No. I mean: the forehead, the back of the head, temples?" Rohmer stressed every word, growing annoyed.

"Everywhere. Or all of them."

"On a scale of 1 to 10, where would you place the intensity of your pain?"

"Don't ask me that. I can't tell. Any physical pain has something metaphysical to it, right? And vice-versa. I don't know whether the intensity expresses the painful sensation or the pain itself. And does the scale you mention go up or down? It's important. I think with you it goes down, while with me it goes up."

"Do you like to socialize?" Rohmer changed the subject, but not before noting something on the observation sheet.

"It bores me."

"What bores you?"

"The emptiness. Formal gatherings."

"Do you have friends?"

"I had more in Romania. In my youth."

"And here?"

"The circle's shrinking."

"What are you afraid of?"

"Uncertainty breeds monsters."

"Monsters that cause headaches?"

"You could put it that way."

"What would those be? Can you name one?"

Only one? The monsters came in groups. Ugly dwarfs who whispered all sorts of threats in Fred's ear.

"Can we talk about something else? I presume that you know all the monsters," Fred confronted him boldly. "After all, this is what you do for living."

"Have you lost weight lately?" the unperturbed Rohmer went on.

"Now that I think about it, yes, I've lost some weight these last months. All the better, right? At my age, any pound lost is a year gained. I don't hear any imperative voices in my head, if that's what you wanted to ask me."

"And your own voice?"

"What about it?" Fred grew interested.

"Do you hear your own voice in your thoughts?"

"I hear my thoughts speaking in my voice."

"And what do they say?"

"Everything I would say out loud if I had the right person in front of me at that moment." The doctor stopped questioning him, and Fred scratched himself irritably.

"My problem is different. Sometimes I speak, I utter words, yet I don't hear my own voice. I was hesitant to tell you this, but now that it came up…"

"Do those you speak to hear you?"

"Not really."

"Is that so?" slipped Rohmer inattentively, making a weak sound, something between a question and an affirmation.

"I'm asked to speak more loudly. I speak louder, but instead of coming out, my voice goes down inside me. It falls into my body. If the other person stuck his ear to my chest or shoulder, he'd probably hear my voice more clearly than I'm able to make it sound through my mouth."

"Do you have an explanation?"

"*I* should have one?" asked Fred, silently enjoying that he had finally been able to nail the great Rohmer, with his glorious diplomas in thick frames, with his notebook drawings where only the screaming peacock was left for them to hear.

"Do you associate these moments with a particular condition?"

"It would be simplistic for me to tie them to my moments of uncertainty or fear. But no, my voice just takes another road sometimes. Or maybe it takes the right path. The body's path. There's a voice of the body too, don't you think?"

"But have you observed when this usually happens? In groups, when you're surrounded by lots of people, or when you're alone, or you have, let's say, an argument with your wife?"

Fred glanced sideways toward Rohmer, who stared at his papers. How much did he know? How well could the doctor read him, and what, exactly, had made him assume such a thing? An argument with his wife! He felt betrayed; it was much too direct a question. On the surface, the discussion between the two had gone nicely till then, pretty equitably. They could easily have exchanged their seats, Fred analyzing the doctor from his ergonomic chair, Rohmer facing him from the other side.

Yet, in essence, Rohmer needs me more than I need him, thought Fred coldly. Another patient, and one who isn't just healthy but with whom he can talk. Though the doctor didn't seem especially eager to talk. If the tables were turned, one would be pulling teeth to get words out of Rohmer. He would surely be a difficult patient. He'd drive you crazy. At least he, Fred, collaborated and opened himself up despite the reservations he had in the beginning and his prejudices regarding the offices of these psychiatrists, psychologists, psychoanalysts, analysts and their couches. Anonymity has its good side too, in the end. In Romania, he would have never-ever agreed to lend himself this way to any doctor, not even if his name were Freud. Everyone knew him there.

Fred decided to ignore Rohmer's allusions to his possible so-called conjugal disputes and push the hide-and-go-seek game farther. He was an expert in this. He had practiced during communism and perfected it only after emigrating to the free world.

"Sometimes, when I talk on the phone, it just so happens that in the middle of the discussion I suddenly hear nothing when I speak. It's like the sound slips down my throat, falls into my stomach or nestles in my heart. But I keep on hearing the person at the other end of the line, his yells into the phone: 'Hello! I can't hear you anymore! Please speak louder! Are you there? Hello!' After that I hear him say: 'We were cut off.' He calls back and says to me: 'I lost you. I don't know what happened; I couldn't hear you anymore. What were you saying?'"

"So, on the telephone, then…"

"Perhaps you want to send me to an ENT specialist?"

Fred smiled ironically, and Rohmer accepted Fred's advantage resignedly.

"But it also happens to me in open spaces." Fred immediately extended him a generous hand, mostly out of the vanity of being listened to. "Perhaps in a hierarchy of questions, *how* is more powerful than *where* or *when*. But I totally agree with you that *why* should be avoided at any cost. A question that is valid only in childhood."

"However, in this situation, I'd insist on *when*," continued Rohmer. "It's important for you to realize in what context, in what conditions, these things happen, *when* you maintain that you'd talk without being heard, or shall we call it the phenomenon of the voice descending into the body."

Fred glanced at him admiringly, professional to professional. What an irony: he had merely come to get some sleeping pills...

"It started to happen after I emigrated. Is it the subconscious fear that I can't get across exactly what I think and feel in a foreign language, despite a vocabulary that's probably richer than the average American's? Or that I can't make myself understood as I'd like to? Either one is possible. In Communist Romania, I made my voice heard loud and clear, though the authorities were trying to silence me. Interesting: in those days it really happened that, often, speaking to a friend on the telephone, we would no longer hear each other. Calls were taped. When the tape recorder ended and the

Secret Service agent on duty wanted to replace it, he'd cut off our conversation so as not to miss anything. But we weren't scared; we taunted them openly. We only told them what they wanted to hear, or what we wanted them to find out. Well, we also talked about books, writers, real life. Unfortunately, they didn't record any of that. They didn't pay attention to what they should have paid the most attention to. Their recordings would have helped us a lot down the road! How many ideas have been lost, how many books were left unwritten!? We depended on them to save our memories, and they betrayed us, so to speak. Many think the Secret Service agents sided with us for the simple reason that they could hear something else, outside of banalities and idiocies. They defended us by making apathetic reports, probably. There was a conspiracy between them and us. A sort of two-way tease, if you will. Like…"

"Interesting," murmured Rohmer, interrupting him, bored.

"Like these last years, here, where no one listened to me anymore. Perhaps that's why I have this feeling that I'm effectively and definitively losing my voice. I have a feeling that silence lurks around me. And it's not like in the old days, when my silences carried weight and meaning, said something, were listened to, minded, even awarded. My silence here is simple; it hides and pretends nothing. What would it be like for thieves to break into your home and attack you, and when you want to cry for help, you open your mouth, unable to utter a single sound? Powerless to defend yourself. Helplessness is much worse than fear."

Rohmer was silent for a second. He then tore a prescription from the pile on the desk, looked over at his own name on the yellow file and proceeded to write.

"I'm a writer," Fred heard his neglected pride saying, or did he merely want to prolong that visit, begun awkwardly and turned upside down unexpectedly?

"Do you write at night?" asked Rohmer flatly, without a shred of curiosity.

"No. No, I can't write at night."

"Lack of inspiration?"

"How do you know?"

"I don't know. I'm asking you."

"For a while it's been harder to go to sleep, that's all."

"How long?"

"Two, three months, I told you. Since then I haven't written anything," he said it more to himself, glancing sideways at the glass bookcase where he saw his shadow reflected in front of the books stacked on the shelves.

"Have you gone through such periods of sleeplessness before?"

"No. I mean yes, right after I emigrated. And more recently, after Mother died. I couldn't come to terms… Thoughts, regrets, for the first time the evidence of death, its material presence so humbling in the end. The first overwhelming defeat."

"Why regrets?"

"She died alone. I know you'll tell me that we all live and die alone."

Rohmer stared at him coldly, perplexed, as if it never crossed his mind to say that.

"She didn't want to come to America. Too much change for one life. Some get their energy from changes; others are drained by them. I was her only child and we were very close. She didn't miss me; she worried about me. She believed in my talent and wanted to see me successful here. In the end, I don't know what caused her disease."

"What disease?"

"A form of depression, from what I gathered; I'm not sure. Psychosis or dementia. Do you think sorrow can cause such a thing?"

It was Rohmer's turn to squint at him, but he maintained his professional expression.

"Anything is possible, but I can't say. I don't know the details."

Rohmer raised his thin eyebrows, which sharpened the already-prominent arches over his eyes.

Fred placed his hand in his breast pocket where he carried his pipe. He took advantage by pressing on his heart, which felt as if it were struggling like a captured pigeon. He felt his head lighten, and a wave of warmth passed through his ears.

"How's your blood pressure?" continued Rohmer monotonously.

"It's been high. Oscillating. I've been on beta-blockers for a year."

The doctor continued to be a good fortune-teller, reading gestures and thoughts. There was no point in opposing him any longer.

"Your cholesterol?"

"I wrote it down there," gestured Fred with his head toward the yellow folder where he had conscientiously answered the entire form, only that Rohmer, instead of going over it, had busied himself with the peacock tail. "A little high, but I'm on a diet. They haven't put me on Lipitor yet. My mother's cholesterol was also a little high, but that's not where I got it from."

"Dreams?"

"I'm sorry?"

He had hoped that the doctor wouldn't ask him now about his ideals. He knew what the doctor was up to; he hadn't been born yesterday.

"Dreams? Everybody has them," Fred answered evasively, sitting more comfortably in his chair. "Some fulfilled, others not."

"Do you have obsessive dreams that return periodically or follow you? Nightmares?"

Eh, here he had to be careful with what he said. People like Rohmer might or might not know what's going on in your noggin, but they're all experts in dreams. Suddenly you get a hell of a diagnosis. But Fred was tempted to answer him; Rohmer seemed too disinterested to be too afraid of him. He tested the waters a bit to see how the discussion would flow.

"I dream of water."

"What kind of water?"

"Water."

"Clean, muddy, how is it?"

"Most of the time muddy."

"And? Is it a river or a sea?"

"It's stale. More like a puddle, so to speak."

"Do you swim? Do you drown? Does it feel like the undercurrent pulls you?"

"No. No, it's not deep water."

"Are you afraid of water?"

"No. I swim well. Since I was a child."

"But are you afraid of the muddy water in the dream?"

"No. I told you, it's not deep."

"Anything else?"

"That's it."

"Fine," said Rohmer intending to close the session.

Fred wasn't ready to leave yet. He came back with details.

"Sometimes I dream of an empty pool with dirty walls. Without water. Or a dry lake. But I keep on swimming. In the emptiness. As if I were flying at low altitude. Or underground."

"Have you ever wanted to hurt yourself?"

"Sometimes you hurt yourself of your own free will. But, naturally, you know all of this. The human universe is complex, but the individual is too simple and lacks complexity. Vanity makes him feel indecipherable, when in reality, to a good reader—and I have no doubt you are one—he's just a book with its pages laid wide-open."

"Thank you," murmured Rohmer confused, and Fred jumped to his rescue.

"I do have another dream, but I don't know whether it's worth mentioning. It doesn't recur often, in any case; much more rarely than the one with water. Sometimes I dream of my own shadow. Dark, like any shadow. And simple. An outline. Sometimes indescribably long and skinny. Other times, absurdly stocky. I know it's still me. Only my outline changes. I make a step toward it, then another, and my shadow runs away from me. I need to try many times to get closer or further until I fit into my shadow exactly. But I can't complain; each time, it fits me perfectly; none of me is left on the outside. But I get up tired; the effort of fitting into my shadow seems to have exhausted me. And yet, luckily, I never lose my shadow; I always catch up to it one way or another."

Fred decided to stop there and fell quiet. Rohmer looked him straight in the eye for the second time. He said nothing and didn't jot anything down on the observation sheet. Fred took his pipe out and twiddled it between his fingers, waiting to see which of them would concede first. Mimi could read dreams too. She would tell you at once: bear means disease. Small child—bad luck. Red color—good news. White roses—wedding. Fish—death. And a falling tooth or a cut tree also meant death in Mimi's interpretations.

"Is there anything else that you'd like to talk about now?"

"What was this all about?"

He had already told the doctor too much. And he couldn't even claim that the doctor had forced it out of him.

"No. Absolutely nothing."

Rohmer handed him the prescription and went back to the peacock tail, which in the meantime had become a surrealist drawing, buried in letters and signs.

"Try to avoid alcohol after taking the pills. I gave you a sleeping pill and an antidepressant. I'll see you in a couple of weeks. It's a new pill, an antidepressant with apparently fewer side effects. I want to see how you react to it."

"Can't you give me enough for a month? I might need more than two weeks' worth. Or can you call the pharmacy to refill my prescription? Do I have to come here again?"

Rohmer ignored his questions.

"Perhaps next time you'll tell me more about the thoughts that keep you from falling asleep. I think you mentioned defeats?"

"Regrets," Fred corrected him, though unsure of what the doctor was referring to.

"And perhaps you could tell me about what you're writing," finished Rohmer, pretending to be interested, and with slightly less energy than in the beginning, stretching out his hand to shake Fred's.

He gets some extra money from insurance, thought Fred, embarrassed by the doctor's suggestion to return to the office so soon. Thanks to Mimi, he had good insurance that covered everything. Including the dentist.

"Long live my business!" Mimi would say. "Otherwise, my dear, if you had your way, we'd have lived under bridges."

It's true—the bridges in New York could really scare anyone, with their gigantic necks stretching between the most coveted island in the world, Manhattan, and boroughs such as Brooklyn and Queens, or the suburbs of New Jersey, where the least lucky lived among traffickers and Mafiosi who paid their bills under the same bridges, crowded with crumbling buildings and dismantled warehouses where gunshots could be heard at night, while drug addicts and stray pigeons gathered daily among trashcans.

In postcards, Brooklyn Bridge looks like a luminous arch between skyscrapers spanning the East River, a magic wand that transformed the dreams of so many immigrants who'd arrived on Ellis Island into a reality, granted a reality sometimes lacking in luster, but the only salvation possible. The bridge was actually a frightening steel structure that, in spite of its monumentality, crushed you instead of uplifting you like all grandiose monuments. But utility and efficiency aren't empty words in America. These bridges bustled with cars and subways above, ships below, pedestrians and bikers on the sides, or miserable folk who plunged into the water, longing to be freed from a lost paradise.

Fred didn't like bridges. They made him feel unsure and dizzy, like all suspended things. Whenever he crossed a bridge, he couldn't wait to get to the other side for fear that the water would engulf him or the cement under his feet might open up and carry him into nothingness. And if he passed under bridges, the sense of panic was even stronger. It was the trepidation, the noise, the fear of the unknown from above, the world that could crash on his head at any point with all its cars, subways and bikers.

Whenever they drove over the George Washington Bridge, he would hesitate until the last moment to decide whether to take the upper or lower level because he could never stop thinking: would it be less painful to die on the bridge or under the bridge? Mimi made the decision every time:

"Take the upper level my dear; at least the view is beautiful!"

With the prescription in his pocket, he regained some of his self-confidence, thanked Rohmer, stepped out and softly closed the door behind him, feeling the flush of a student who's fooled his professor, or a schemer whose farce worked out. Fear and histrionics had always been his favorite themes. Anxiety was one of his new ones. The loss of reality. All of it was a gold mine for writing. Where does the being end, and the spirit begin?

By the time he got out, it had started to rain. His headache throbbed in the clean spring air. His forehead and eyes felt heavy as lead. Perhaps he should have spoken to Rohmer more seriously about these migraines; perhaps Mimi was right to ask where they came from, having become ever more frequent and more violent? But Rohmer had understood something, or he wouldn't have prescribed that antidepressant along with the sleeping pills. Which Fred wouldn't take anyway. This is all these psychiatrists know; as soon as they catch you, they put you on some pills. Further down the road, whoever can, makes it, with or without the pills. Some change their personalities, others find peace but lose their emotions. Artists lose their sensitivity; guilty people become indifferent and victims develop a sense of guilt, criminals weep, cynics laugh hysterically.

One day he had come across a site on the Internet promoting a sort of food that was found to cure loneliness and depression: macaroni with cheese. Beneath a dish with yellowish pasta covered in butter, there were calls by nutritionists and psychiatrists enlisted by the advertising agency saying that macaroni with cheese makes you happy. Fat and happy. They'd even found out that thin people get depressed more easily than the overweight who are jovial and content, encouraged to be comfortable with their own bodies, free from any sort of complex. Consumption must be encouraged at any cost; a joyful and prosperous society, in which pathological consumption combats the pathologies of the mind.

On the same day, a TV presenter said that shopping is therapeutic, especially if you pay cash, and a

Harvard professor with a gray beard and a white coat pompously confirmed the benefits of shopping for one's self-esteem and its positive influence on curing any sort of psychosis.

No point trying to catch a cab. When it rains the city loses control, as if the signal has just been given for predetermined chaos through which some of its accumulated energies could escape. The taxis pile up honking at the stop lights; people flank the edges of sidewalks with upraised hands trying to flag a cab though all the cabs are suddenly occupied or off duty; hot dog carts run down the street; shady people quickly pack up their stands with counterfeit watches and purses; uniformed door men whistle desperately in front of hotels holding huge umbrellas above their clients' heads in the hopes of a fat tip; cops also whistle at intersections, while tourists hide under store awnings, not knowing which way to go.

Fred raised his elegant woolen coat collar, more to protect himself against the migraine than the light rain, and he stopped by a group of refugees under a Bloomingdale's roof, once Mimi's favorite store.

Jim was a stone's throw away from there. Once a successful sculptor and a Woodstock survivor, Jim had changed into a mediocre painter, and after his marriage to a capricious and snobbish member of the bourgeoisie who'd had the timely decency to pass over to that other world, he remained in their beautiful apartment on the Upper East Side, where he had improvised a studio filled with canvases, colors, useless objects and eternal residue from the previous days' parties.

Fred couldn't help visiting him, even though Mimi had bluntly told him to come home immediately because she expected FedEx to bring an express order for her Spa. He had to sign for delivery. It's the least he could do. But all Fred *could* do was call the doorman of the apartment complex where they had been comfortably living for fifteen years—since Mimi hit the jackpot with her business—and ask him to receive the package and sign on his behalf, hinting that a fine tip would come his way.

Although not exactly his cup of tea, Jim brought him a breath of fresh air—freedom, humor and genuineness, with shades of decadence and bohemianism, an atmosphere that he sometimes missed. But not for long. Jim emanated both, power and failure, wasted talent and ill-fated adventure, just enough to make Fred need to take a sneak peek in the mirror, unable to face the image of failure straight in the eye.

Jim's attractiveness could also be explained through the fact that he reminded Fred of his own youth in Romania. They were good years because the blood flowed vigorously through his veins, women were enticing and accessible, he dreaded disappearing into a world without chances and this made him live all the more intensely, burning the candle at both ends. The system, opaque and oppressive as it was, had not been able to inhibit either Jim or himself—quite the contrary, their senses had sharpened. Having nothing, they had nothing to lose, so they exposed themselves to all sorts of excesses, with the rebellious feeling that they would keep on thinking, creating, making passionate utopian plans in spite of those plotting their funerals.

The parties never ended, in the painters' studios, in the apartments or restaurants of the writers' guild, in pubs and taverns drowned in cigarette smoke, or at the home of some member of the Communist Party elite, more open-minded, who longed for the company of exclusive intellectuals, whom he'd feed on the one hand, and observe to see what was in their mind the other. It's true that many of his drinking buddies—a serious job in the artistic field—died pretty young from cirrhosis or heart attack.

"Well, Fred, we're the true adventurers, not your kind who've gone here and there. I know you've come from nothing, good for you, but the hard thing isn't to start from scratch in a normal world, but to go on in the nightmare that is here. From one misery to another. Freedom has come with its wild capitalism and now we rip each other apart," a former colleague from Animafilm Studio, that went bankrupt after the revolution, once wrote to him.

But Fred had kept an idyllic memory of his old world, frozen in time. He was happy there, as it was. His first loves, his mother still aware and powerful, the manly assurance that he was doing something important. There had been frankness in communication and a genuine culture, though one of poverty and despair. All that generated ideas and created passive forms of artistic resistance.

He had left Romania a year before the fall of communism, thanks to one of those absurd situations that destiny sometimes sets up. He wasn't among those who had planned their flight ahead of time, strategized to confront every risk, hardened by the miseries of life and the lack of perspective. He had kept his fond memories rather than resentments and continued to believe that the exile he had chosen had been the seed of an event that he would not cease to dissect throughout the years that followed. To what extent can we go against the wave that carries us from behind and pushes us along a certain path?

In an interview he did by phone in New York for the Romanian National Radio station a few years after Ceaușescu's fall, a reporter asked him whether now, living in freedom, he would still leave Romania. Fred hesitated to answer directly, saying instead that: "...to feel free is to know how to keep your mind clear and your soul healthy, and this depends on your internal resources, even if you live in a desert, on a deserted island or behind barbed wire. Freedom is each person's power to find a method of survival in a political or geographical context, to modify and dominate the external world through personal strengths. This means neither adapting to a foul place nor making shameful compromises in a particular system. Freedom is the tenacity to save yourself spiritually under any condition, and that is worth fighting for. To each their own fight. I write; I've tried to get closer to the truth rather than rebel against daily realities."

Had he felt oppressed as a Jew in Romania? The reporter went on, ignoring the confessional connotations of Fred's answer and his fair and direct attitude.

"No more than anyone else," said Fred undisturbed.

The criticisms came soon enough: The arrogance of the one who lives elsewhere... The Jews who brought communism over, have come to power in Eastern Europe, milked the system and saved themselves, emigrating to get to the top again in their adoptive countries... A writer who was up-and-coming produced nothing interesting and immigrated... Also, an activist's son. They immediately remembered that his father was an illegal fighter in the civil war in Spain against Franco and had been buried in the Jewish section at Bellu cemetery in Bucharest, with the hammer and sickle—the Communist symbol—carved upon his headstone.

But Fred's rebellion against malicious reactions faded over time. No matter how defeated he felt, Fred wasn't the sort of person to grow bitter. There was always a secret box that he thought he could open whenever he wished.

A Romanian writer living in Paris, a winner of prizes and fame, disgusted beyond words by Ceauşescu's regime and the country's decline, had once said to him, while sipping on oysters at a bistro in The Marais:

"The country of birth, more than anything, means the language; in the end, a writer immigrates not to a foreign country, but into a foreign language. An exiled writer has only this inheritance. The language of birth is his weakness, but also his strength. And, in the end, his only ally."

Fred agreed quickly. He had just arrived in Paris, enjoyed the city, met old friends and new people in the literary world. He had been highly successful in Romania, and the exiles' woes didn't interest him much. He neither meant to stay in Paris too long nor flee elsewhere. But he listened to the man until the end:

"No matter how successful an exiled creator becomes, he wants to be acknowledged in his homeland. A subconscious satisfaction, a sort of revenge against all the torment of starting all over in a foreign culture that doesn't care for strangers, a feeling not unlike wanting to make one's mother proud of one's achievements. And let me tell you something else: posterity only exists in your country of birth."

Fred was surprised to hear this from someone who didn't seem to need the approval of a minor culture like Romanian that, over and above all, had rejected him. It seemed to him a frivolous affirmation, a whim more than anything. *He only wants to improve his track record*, thought Fred. Who cares about posterity? Only the defeated live with the hope of acknowledgment after death. Better to keep your duplicity going and pretend you've made it and be thankful for small successes than to wait to defy eternity, merely to camouflage your failure. He couldn't imagine the phantoms that would soon come to haunt him as well.

Satisfied with the idea of visiting Jim, he defied the rain and crossed Lexington Avenue by Laura Lee boutique, a store where Mimi used to order him expensive shirts and silk scarves ("From now on we have to cut down expenses, dear, all's unsure, who knows what the future has in store for us!"), threw a dollar in the plastic cup that a beggar held over his shaggy dog, went to CVS to get the prescription for his troublesome sleeping pills filled, bought two *Tylenol* pills which he swallowed in front of the cashier, and collided against the automatic door while trying to make way for an old lady with purple hair. And then he walked toward Park Avenue with the feeling that life could be picked up right where he left off.

Where had Fred left his life? In his insomniac nights he obsessively relived his way from Bucharest to Paris and, finally, to New York. From there, there was nowhere to go.

"Final station. Terminus," Mimi had told him as soon as they landed at Kennedy Airport almost 20 years earlier. "This is what I wanted. I struggled to get here and I won't let this good fortune go away. I'll be someone, mark my words." Mimi threatened him with her playful eyes, tearing up with ambition. "I won't embarrass you,

you'll see. You'll win the Nobel Prize and I'll win the lottery. A great writer like you deserves a wife worthy of him. I want to help you fulfill your dream."

"The hardest thing to cope with is a fulfilled dream," Fred managed to whisper before getting into his cousin's car, but Mimi had stopped listening to him. She was already dizzy from thinking about the metropolis that awaited her and the success that she would strive for with all her might.

Fred had crouched on the back seat, while Mimi, seated in the front seat by his cousin, dominated the conversation by speaking ceaselessly, excited even by the fairly desolate neighborhoods bordering Queens. In retrospect, that road seemed the beginning of the end. While Fred sank in the back, Mimi's neck strained with curiosity. He grew smaller as she grew taller, as if they had both sipped from a miraculous drink that caused opposite effects.

"Isn't it fantastic?" Mimi had asked as they drove onto the Queensboro Bridge and Manhattan suddenly appeared before them like a charcoal drawing on the horizon, with its bold yet warm architecture in the orange twilight, on that September when their lives were about to start over, unexpectedly, like that unique city on the edge of the Atlantic.

As they neared Manhattan, the sky became more of a surrealist painting, the sun having shattered, scattering itself like egg yolk mixed by a fork above the skyscrapers. A prophetic sky for those who knew how to read the signs of the sky, but in those days neither of them cared to decipher the clues that nature might send when one is at a crossroads.

"New York, New York," hummed Mimi next to his cousin, who was amused by his young relative. Fred would have liked to have slept—a sort of defense mechanism—slept for a long time, as in his childhood when he felt protected. But his first night in New York coincided with his first bout of insomnia.

Edi, a tiny man with thick glasses, slightly over 40, lived on the ground floor of an apartment building in a Jewish neighborhood in Brooklyn. He worked at a bank a few blocks from his home. He wasn't married and didn't seem like he'd find his soul mate anytime soon. He was normal-looking and unconcerned about his looks. He wore the same dark suit with white shirts with striped ties when he went to the bank, and at home he wore the same brown pullover, loose on one of its sides with a button dangling stubbornly. In the winter he wore a tight coat with short sleeves, inherited from his grandfather. The question is open as to whether he kept it for sentimental reasons, negligence, comfort or stinginess.

Edi showed them the apartment, stressing the advantages of American kitchens to Mimi, from the microwave and dishwasher to the coffee machine and blender. He pulled the kitchen drawers out, letting them close slowly, while watching her, satisfied.

"They have wheels and close slowly. This doesn't exist in Europe yet."

Mimi rolled her eyes and subtly chuckled with Fred, who had asked her to be understanding of his cousin's habits and strangeness.

"Can we turn off the air conditioning? I can't stand the cold," said Fred.

Edi shook him off categorically.

"No way! I can't live without it. You haven't discovered comfort yet. You come from Paris, but Paris is still in Europe."

"Have you been there?" asked Mimi sulkily.

"Never. I don't care for it. Europe doesn't exist for me. All I know is that it's time-worn, filled with nationalists and anti-Semites."

Mimi would have liked to argue with him, but Fred glanced at her, telling her to cut it out. Edi was doing them a great favor hosting them; they didn't know how long they'd need to stay at the apartment, and there was no need to argue with him.

Edi gave them his bedroom and slept on the couch in the living room, a large and dark room shaded by a bushy willow that covered the window. From there, Fred would scrutinize the new world in the coming months. On Saturday, the streets were filled with families dressed in black, going to and coming from synagogue. The men wore kippahs or hats, suits and traditional payot; the women wore long skirts, veils or little hats, and the children imitated their parents' tastes in clothing. Fred looked at them from his bedroom window, which faced the boulevard, and if it weren't for the squirrels that chased each other in the trees, he would have had the impression that an entire Israeli neighborhood had been transplanted to Brooklyn. There were synagogues, Jewish recreational centers, yeshivas and kosher restaurants, and special elevators were programmed to stop on every floor for those who lived on the upper stories to use without having to press any buttons on the Sabbath.

Edi had worked in a diamond kibbutz in Netanya, near Tel Aviv, come to America very young, and other than his managerial position at the bank, was involved in a business on 47th Street that he told no one about. He used to come home from work around 6:00 PM, eat something standing up by his kitchen sink, and then he'd take his knapsack and leave for Manhattan about the time when the jewelry stores put their goods in safes, pulled the bars on the windows and began to count their earnings in the backrooms.

Edi's ability to polish diamonds was second to none. He'd come home around 10:00 PM, turn on the TV and sink into his couch exhausted, with an empty expression and automatic gestures. He didn't go to movies or the theater; he only went to a restaurant if there was some party organized by the bank or an anniversary.

"He's on cruise control. If you move his couch and desk to the moon, he won't even notice it; he'll keep the same daily routine. He's a cog in the machine: until the mechanism stops, he'll keep at it. And the mechanism seems well-oiled," commented Mimi, starting to understand the myth of work in America that Europeans criticized sarcastically but whose results they envied.

Edi never went on vacation anywhere and hadn't visited Israel after he moved to America; and as for Romania, where he'd been born, had a vague recollection, mostly from his parents' stories. They'd left when he was 9 under the agreement Ceaușescu made with the state of Israel, which set the confiscation of goods and a payment of $5,000 for every Jew in exchange for the right to emigrate.

His mother had died from cancer and his father died on a bus one morning on his way to work when a suicide bomber blew himself up for $5,000 that Saddam Hussein had promised to pay his family, plus a guaranteed spot in heaven.

Edi had been well-behaved and ambitious. As a result, the kibbutz helped him go to America, and the Jewish community there helped him get a job. He rarely laughed and when he did, he laughed clumsily, mostly with his shoulders, but he had an inadvertent serene smile as if he were always thinking about something else or something in particular—God knows what.

"And where will Fred write?" asked Mimi.

There was no desk or table in the house outside of the one in the kitchen. Edi shrugged.

"I don't know. He can go across the road to the library."

"It doesn't work that way," Mimi insisted. "You don't write according to a schedule. What library? You can't do it if there are people around. He doesn't write bills but novels! He needs solitude, atmosphere…"

Fred stood by the door and coughed nervously, hinting that it wasn't the right time to demand too much. Edi ignored Mimi's comments.

"And I'm going to ask you, Fred, to go behind the apartment complex when you want to smoke your pipe. Ah, and if you want, I go swimming in the morning at the yeshiva's sports complex across the street; you can come too. I can bring a guest. Only that you have to get up before 6:00 AM."

Mimi and Fred exchanged glances.

"I only got up that early when I was in the army. And only when they pulled me out of the bed, sheets and all. But thank you for the invitation," Fred smiled. "I'm not really the athletic type. In Romania I played tennis, and in Paris I started to take long walks. And I'm not such a morning person. I read and write until late."

"Do you have any money?" Edi wanted to know on that first evening, before turning off the TV as a hint that it was time for them to retreat to their bedroom.

They answered at the same time.

"We have enough," said Fred.

"We have some," whispered Mimi.

They had $500 that remained after they'd paid the last month's rent in Paris and the plane tickets. They also had a diamond ring from Fred's mother that they'd been told to sell if none of their plans went their way.

Since their first day in America, Fred had chosen to play the second fiddle in the couple. He allowed Mimi to ask all the questions, to make sense of things, to explore the neighborhood and the possibility of finding a temporary job; and Mimi, who was playfully excited as a squirrel all day, had befriended several neighbors and knew where to buy the cheapest goods. She got to know the subway system and collected a stack of flyers about plays, cruises on the Hudson, museum programs, coupons and promotional vacation offers, for when they'd be able to live normally and afford these luxuries.

"My love, Manhattan is *the only place* to be. Everything happens there," Mimi used to say.

"Don't mention to Edi that; he'll get upset."

"I couldn't care less about Edi's suffering. And I think he feels great here. It's his place. But we have to live *there*. You deserve that. I can just see you writing in a studio with windows facing Central Park. On a high floor, of course."

Mimi's inoffensive snobbishness and ambitiously lofty dreams, her desire to do everything in her power to break ranks under the pretext that he deserved the best, amused Fred. She moved slowly her round, delicate ass under her short jean skirt; she walked on every surface like a gazelle wary of hurting her fragile ankles; she wore her hair in a ponytail and her nose pointed up, and she told everyone that she was a ballerina and her husband was a famous writer who would win New York over one day. And everyone believed her.

On an evening when Fred was reading and lying down in the bedroom, Mimi came to the door of the apartment carrying a beautiful rosewood desk. Igor, the Ukrainian super whom she befriended, had given her a tip that on every Wednesday evening people put stuff out to be picked up by the garbage trucks the next morning; she might find all kinds of things there, from carpets, televisions and vacuums to furniture, some in excellent condition.

Igor had even offered to help her with his old but sizable car, and that's how they were lucky enough to come across a desk that Mimi immediately declared was perfect for Fred. She and the super carried it and set it up in the bedroom under the window, while Fred stared at it perplexedly. Mimi then invited Igor for a shot of vodka in the kitchen.

"It's done! Now you have a desk: go write!" ordered Mimi, with a triumphant gaze.

"What will Edi say?" asked Fred anxiously, ignoring her order to go write. "We can't just crash into his life like this after the favor he's doing us."

"What can he say? After all, we're furnishing his apartment? Don't you see what everything looks like around here? I think he got these odd pieces of wood from the streets too."

When Edi came home that night, Mimi welcomed him in the hallway with a smile. She performed a pirouette in her irresistible skirt and rolled her talented actress' eyes, and told him that she had decided that his place needed a transformation from looking like an apartment that belonged to an old bachelor, busy with the daily rigors of work. Edi looked at her indifferently and smiled, as if he'd allow her to do anything she pleased; it didn't matter to him.

"I bet that if I hadn't told him, he wouldn't even have noticed that a desk had just sprouted in his room. Doesn't he seem a bit of a lunatic?"

"He's a very decent man, Mimi. That's all there is to it. Not everyone can be as alert as you are."

"Hmm," said Mimi doubtfully, "I hate passive men."

For the first time, Fred felt an electric current shoot down his spine. Might he be one of them?

Since he'd come to New York, he'd spent most of his time reading, taking notes in a little pocketbook with a blue cover for the book he'd eventually write, and he only went out to take walks and to smoke his pipe at night. When he did go out, he walked prudently and heavily, as if he wanted to see how solid the cement on which Mimi hopped and clattered ceaselessly was. When they took strolls together, she was even excited by the amount of trash gathered in black plastic bags on the edge of sidewalks on the curb.

"Consumption here is no joke! Wealth can also be measured by how much is thrown out, don't you think?"

They approached the city differently. Sometimes Mimi's excitement amused him; other times it irritated him. Fred seemed to embrace the city gently; he was still exploring from a distance, touching it discreetly and pulling back his finger swiftly when it seemed that the wide mouth of a whale would open up, ready to swallow him unchewed.

"What I like here is that people are friendly," Mimi said to him. "They smile at me, they ask me how I'm doing, they tell me to have a good day and to take care of myself."

"Do you think they care outside of these polite phrases?"

"I don't know and it doesn't matter. They make me feel good. I'm sure it'll be easier than in Paris."

Fred smiled skeptically, and Mimi threw her handbag on her shoulder and went out to conquer Manhattan.

For several weeks she had tried, unsuccessfully, to obtain a position as a ballerina. She'd been to dozens of auditions and gotten in touch with agents and producers, who'd thank her, wish her a good day and to take care of herself, and offer her nothing. Maybe it was her age? At the end of the day she decided that she would make do temporarily with working as a receptionist at a beauty salon in Soho.

They lived in a sort of provisional stability. Mimi earned something and Fred worked on his book. He picked her up from work every night and they wandered through the art galleries of Soho. Mimi made grand plans for the future—how they'd decorate their home, what paintings and furniture they'd buy. Sometimes they ate at an inexpensive restaurant in the Village, and they went to a movie or a show when they were lucky enough to find cheap tickets. And every night, Mimi asked him how much more he'd written that day. She'd sulk whenever Fred told her he hadn't had a good day and hadn't advanced too far.

"My love, I don't understand. Now that you have peace and a desk, why can't you write?"

"I write, Mimi, I write, but not always on paper. But I think about my writing all the time. I write in my thoughts first. Sometimes frantically; the words come in battalions, stampede each other, contradict each other, and then I erase everything with the intent of starting all over. I've written so many wonderful pages in my mind! And when the time comes, I'll put them down on paper."

"Whatever," Mimi gave in, without allowing herself to get intimidated by him. "Let's say that in Paris I understood you weren't in the mood… Only that, at the end of the day, you have to finish that book, right? So move on with your writing!"

"You imagine that as soon as I turn on the faucet, ideas just flow?"

"Yes, that's how it should be. And let me read what you've written till now."

"When I finish the first chapter, I'll show it to you," Fred brushed her off, trying to change the subject, but Mimi was a fiery Aries who didn't stop until she made her point no matter what.

"Just so you know, I also have good ideas for your writing," she assured him, whispering in a more relaxed tone and shaking her blonde ponytail.

Fred walked through Edi's apartment like a lion in a cage, tapping his pipe, undecided how to start the book and unsure of the tone that he'd adopt for his potential new public, or he'd read for hours on end by the window with the feeling that books and solitude offered his only final protection. Only that solitude was different than loneliness.

It was loneliness that had terrified his mother who had stayed back in Bucharest; the loneliness that his friend Sam had cultivated as a refuge from an empty life; the loneliness that for Mimi had become merely an empty word, suspended like a bug caught in a spider's web; the loneliness that he instinctively tried to avoid during these years of emigration, but now he could feel the space around him grow empty, and the air and walls tighten, shrinking his shadow—his shadow, filled with the residue from so many changes.

Mimi kept the apartment clean and did the cooking. She knew all kinds of soup recipes from her mother, and she'd learned how to make delicate sauces with butter and herbs at the restaurant where she'd worked in Paris. She always enticed Edi with something warm "just like mother's cooking," but he grimaced moodily. He had grown used to his salads, his sandwiches in plastic containers on which he spread mayonnaise, and fast food in cardboard containers that he drowned in ketchup, turning Mimi's stomach.

"What's wrong with this guy?" Mimi asked Fred.

"Nothing, Mimi. He's adapted to this world, that's all."

"Well, at least he's not religious Orthodox. That would be all we needed!"

On some mornings, Fred would go to the library across the street. One morning, a flyer on the library's bulletin board that announced the week's events and programs caught his eye. A librarian position had been posted, and he wanted to go to the interview that was scheduled in a few days. Mimi exploded:

"A librarian in a neighborhood library? In Brooklyn? Are you kidding? It's degrading. You're an artist, a refined intellectual; how can you do this? And when will you have time to write your books? Isn't it enough that I work?"

"But I have to do something. I can't stay home like this."

"Who tells you to stay? Write!"

"Mimi, stop patronizing me."

"Have patience, my love," purred Mimi with a languorous voice, feeling that she had gone too far. She opened up his shirt-buttons and pulled off her T-shirt, revealing her breasts, cold and luscious apples that Fred's palms rubbed greedily. "Just write! Things will get better soon. I foresee a miracle. We only need to draw it toward us."

"And what should we do to draw it?" said Fred, devouring her with his eyes.

"It's important for us to want something very much and then to visualize it as if it were real, to enjoy it as if we already had it, and hocus pocus, it'll happen."

"Where did this idea come from?"

"I read an article in a magazine about the unlimited power of the mind. Auto-suggestion can have earth-shaking effects. It seems that you can get anything you want if you know how to ask."

"Meaning: knock and a door shall be opened to you, ask and you shall receive?"

"Yes. I'd like to take a class, something…"

"A class on miracles?"

"Don't laugh. I want to get some books. I'd like to read more about this."

"You'd do better to read Kafka. Or Borges."

"Let Kafka be. I'm over that era. I need something practical now," Mimi sulked again.

"Practical? I thought you were talking about miracles. I thought you wanted to fly headlong into the esoteric."

"Fred, here people believe in magic."

"Here, in Brooklyn?"

"No need to laugh at me. I'm convinced that a miracle will happen. And we deserve it, don't we? We're beautiful young people. Isn't that so, Fred?" she said playfully, studying his reaction. "You a genius, me wonderful. We love each other," she purred, and her palms made their way under his tight shirt. She caressed his back lightly with her long nails, went down beneath his belt and pressed against him, her body sticking to his. "We do love each other, right?"

She pushed him toward the bedroom, crisscrossing her skillful legs with his, as in the steps to an Argentinian tango. Fred smiled, a little frightened of being hit where it hurt most, and let himself be rolled onto the bed, bit, licked, his clothes taken off. He turned her on her back while she encircled him with her legs and held him tight until she felt him penetrate her. She rubbed the tip of her nose against his left earlobe, knowing this excited him the most, as Fred kneaded her breasts and thighs, moaning heavily.

Mimi usually finished impetuously, struggling like a wild cat on a leash, trying to restrain her moans while Edi slept in the living room.

In the morning, she unleashed herself as soon as she heard the key turning in the front door. It almost became a habit. As soon as Edi went to swim, Mimi would grope beneath the covers toward Fred's penis and massage it expertly, especially on the sensitive tip. She would lie on top, and propping her hands on Fred's shoulders, ride him frantically, cry, pant and let out all sorts of sounds before collapsing on him, exhausted as if she had conquered a fortress. She'd take a shower, and gratified, leave for the beauty parlor where she'd use the most sensuous whisper on the telephone:

"Hello. *Soho Fancy.* How may I help you?"

Fred found Jim thoroughly destroying his last painting, the same one he had described to Fred only two days prior as being his best to date. His large palms with wide nails—sculptor's or criminal's nails—cracked and covered with paint, flailed in the air like the wings of fighting roosters.

"I should have stayed with stone and wood," yelled Jim, putting the coup de grace to his ruined work. "Where is the consistency of form? Shall we fight all our lives with the illusion that light will fall in a perfect angle each time?"

Jim addressed Fred behind him, continuing his mental discourse out loud.

Fred tossed his jacket over a box full of empty wine bottles and felt the noise in his brain quiet down. Jim's logorrhea perfectly covered up the droning of his thoughts which were unable to assume a coherent form in words to be uttered. Perhaps the therapist that Mimi once forced him to see might be a solution. Fred had treated that one with the same resistance as the psychiatrist he saw that morning: he had refused to lie down on the couch, sat stiffly and answered ambiguously, but in the end, the therapist's tactics had unknotted, if not his tongue, at least some of his tangled thoughts. The fact that he was talking about other things, avoiding thinking about himself was good for him. Something else, an escape from the terror that nothing remains after you draw the line.

In a corner of the large room, a tiny Asian woman, stretched out on a hole-ridden mattress, leafed through a magazine. He greeted her with an indistinct murmur, but the woman didn't look at him; she only pulled the dirty sheet over her bare back, because of cold rather than shame, reached out to the DVD player on the floor and turned the music on louder; very loud, as a signal that she didn't want to socialize. Perfect, sighed Fred, relieved. Vangelis' *Sauvage* tickled his just-relaxed neurons. He tried to attune himself to its regal tonalities, sounds raised toward the absolute or down to hell, as if a cathedral were being torn from the earth and dashed against a cliff.

"Turn that damn music down," yelled Jim to the woman. "Do you want to crack our skulls open now? Look at her, she doesn't have any idea what she's listening to. God knows what drove me to tell her I liked this CD... For the last two days that's all she's been playing. If you tell her to do something, she goes with it to the bitter end. Asiatic servility, a sort of obsessive-compulsive devotion. But if you give her the cold shoulder, wham, you're in for it! These Asians pretend to be humble only to study you better, just like the wolf in *Little Red Riding Hood*, and as soon as they catch you, they club you. The future is theirs, mark my words. Don't you see what's happening? They put rats in our food, mercury in our fish, botulism in can-food, lead in toys and cancer in medicine. We don't produce anything anymore: everything's made in China, while we're indebted to them for hundreds of years. And we also apparently export millions of tons of scrap metal to them. They're building their empire on our ruins. We're inattentive, superficial, sophisticated; they're quiet, they keep on digging patiently, and one day they'll burst out and eat us alive. And, what's more, we're the ones who gave them the tools. Anyway, in bed it's different, I won't complain. Small and thin as they are, these Asian girls know what they're doing."

Fred glanced embarrassed at the woman who didn't seem to be paying any attention to him.

"Don't look at her! She's not deaf; she just doesn't understand anything. She speaks English as if she were eating toothpicks. Do you know what she said yesterday to a friend who came here? 'Nice weather!' he told her. 'Nice weather to you too!' she said. I think these folks have their brains wired differently. Or they come from another planet. Do you want me to give you proof of their giant leap forward, which happened right before our eyes? In their country, they ate dogs, and now you see rich Chinese women walking their Pekinese on leashes on Madison Avenue. This is what they've come to! We chase terrorists in the mountains of Afghanistan, and these Asians terrorize us elegantly from a distance, conquer us little by little, molecule by molecule, cent by cent. Lord, what an irresponsible country we live in! We keep our doors and windows open for everyone to come in, just like a brothel! This is why what happened to us happened. And we still learn nothing. We watch how our country is taken away and we do nothing. We'll go to the dogs. I've been saying this for a while!"

Fred wasn't in the mood for this. He knew all of his friend's racist and extreme theories, but all those thoughts softened as soon as they passed through the bed.

"Do you have anything else to tell me?"

"Would you like a vodka?" And before Fred could answer, Jim filled himself a glass and guzzled it.

"I have a horrible headache," whispered Fred.

"Exactly. This helps. *A vodka in its time is like ten ladies in their prime.*"

"It's too much."

"Do you want to go out? There's an exhibition at the gallery on 57th and then we're going to eat something."

"How about her?" asked Fred looking at the woman.

"Don't worry about her. She'll sniff some crack and snooze till I get back."

Jim put on a vest with pockets of all sizes, right over his undershirt, took the keys and winked to the woman, who answered with an ambiguous smile. He opened the door and let Fred leave first, then closed the door behind them.

"What is it with your headaches?" he asked as he stomped on the stairs with his military boots.

"I don't know. Spring asthenia maybe, as they used to say in Romania. I just can't sleep."

"And Madam Mimi does nothing?" insinuated Jim with a smirk.

"No, that's not it," Fred hedged.

Mimi detested Jim for two reasons. For one, because he exhibited a virility that was hard to resist and that stirred her instincts, making her seem an easily available woman and revealing her true nature, which she'd fought against for years. On the other hand, she disliked him because of the influence he seemed to have on Fred.

"You don't like my friends," Mimi reproached him. "Either they're snobs with money or empty and have nothing to say, in your words. And they don't know what to do to get on your good side. Can't you see that in this world, if you don't have money, you're nothing? And what? Do they have to be uncultivated if they're rich?"

"No, but your friends are."

"On the other hand, you've surrounded yourself with losers, arrogant folks who rationalize their failures in pretentious words. You're not one of them. Get that into your head: you're a creator par excellence, you are cut out for a champion, not for a drowned-in-alcohol-and-marijuana loser, like that nobody Jim," said Mimi.

Lately, Fred noticed that her discourse had gained new nuance:

"Go to Jim. You feel at home over there. He'll tell you just how noble it is to be a failure, how God damned wonderful it is to not be able to produce anything except words in this world."

"But I live on words."

"Let's be serious. You live on my money. From what I've seen, your words haven't come to amount to two cents."

"You used to treasure them in the old days, and you used to treasure me," Fred tight roped between irony and the fear of another attack that might commence at any time.

"Look, the problem is, Fred, I'm no longer the girl you can turn persuade with quotations and empty promises. I read those books too; I understood what there is to understand and moved on with my life. You've mired yourself in mud all these years, have done nothing but sink. This little girl's grown up, honey. You can't fool her anymore by flaunting that image of glory faded. I took you seriously; I still treasure you for what you might have been, but I no longer buy those silly stories over which you and Jim and Sam's friends get drunk. I don't have time for that."

"What is time, Mimi, if not a crack in a wall? An open eye in a fence, big enough to give you the feeling that you're slipping out of the cage you've been locked in since birth. A convention that separates order from disorder, the distance between zero and one. Do you follow? The inability to be eternal."

Mimi rolled her eyes as Fred took his notebook out to jot down some ideas that he would never make use of.

"I'd follow you, but I have no reason to anymore. I know all your idiocies inside-out." Mimi drowned herself in fury. "Stop trying to be a smartass. I'll tell you what time is, in my own words: void. Why the hell shouldn't you split hairs about time when you have all the time in the world? What else do you have to do? No worries. Mimi will work since she's the dumber one; that's all she can do; you keep on going with your hallucinations and pills. And what do I get from you in exchange for all that? Ah? What kind of joy? You don't even want to go to shows anymore: they might bore you, God forbid. We don't travel anymore. What's the point when you can imagine it all?! There are neither places nor happenings, only thoughts, right? Reality is illusory and we can turn it whichever way we please. Can't you see that I, too, have learned this lesson by heart? Well, if that's how it goes, why don't you turn it all around, in your favor? Why didn't you make this illusion come true and write and publish your books? Ah? No one comes to visit us anymore, because they're tired of your bitter and superior attitude. And I don't want them to see you in one of those moods. You know what I'm talking about; don't make me tell you."

"I don't make you do anything," Fred whispered, and that's when Mimi began to shoot innuendos:

"Too bad. I liked it when you made me. Subdued me. Bed's like a library now. And me? What should I do? Our life's going to hell."

The dialogue stopped abruptly, and a fog suddenly covered Fred's mind.

"Let's walk around; I don't feel like a show right now," he said to Jim, whose eyes were staring at the legs of a blonde in high heels walking ahead of them.

It was obvious that the heels were dreadfully painful, but women enjoy torturing themselves, according to Jim.

"I agree. Anyway, it wasn't a big deal: a guy with money but no talent who paints for those who have even more money. Nantucket landscapes with coarse colors, or some feeble nautical scenery, claiming to inspire good feelings. Art begins where reality ends. This is the first lesson. But I haven't learned it properly either."

The blonde shook her hair with a nervous gesture. She walked like a wobbling stork with her legs too thin and too long. She seemed to poke the air with half-bare breasts beneath a tight black blouse. Behind her, Jim salivated with pleasure. Fred avoided gazing in her direction. She reminded him of Mimi in the old days, after she'd stepped out of her ballet slippers and into the thin high heels that she would never-ever give up. As a young girl, she'd been obsessed with the idea that she was too short, and in America she decided that you can't be a true lady if you don't look men in the eye, at the same level, so the high heels had entered into the requisites for her debut, her nouveau riche transformation into a member of her new world. The shoes' rhythmic threatening noise, as if they were ripping the world apart, now scared Fred.

Jim always went on the defense. He sniffed the woman's scent, only to say later on that it had choked him:

"Why can't these chicks be natural? Why do they always have to defy, to pretend, to display something outside of who they really are? In short, they act like unhappy creatures that struggle to show a triumphant image. What matters most to them isn't how they live but how they're perceived. Forever restlessness and on alert, looking in the mirror on all possible sides, neurotic, smelling fresh blood and naiveté from afar, ready to throw themselves upon any victim and devour it on the pretext that they're actually saving it. They provoke wars only to give men the chance to win them. Or to kill one another."

He sometimes added:

"And after every war, the matriarchy! The history of humanity is actually a long series of matriarchies. And after all of these matriarchies, they've still got the know-how to victimize themselves. They'll amaze us for another thousand years with their legendary suffering. Eh, let it be. Now, political correctness has given them the power. Let's see what they'll come up with!"

The rain had stopped, and Fifth Avenue shined. A piece of sky was divided by a plane; seen from below, the plane seemed to fly from one window to another between two skyscrapers that confronted each other's height, like two dragons having risen from cement. Fred ignored Jim's comments, no reason to fight with him. He had his own monsters to fight with, playing in his head. The migraine became even stronger. Jim changed the tone as he always did when he felt he was losing Fred's attention.

"God, what a city! How can people live anywhere else but here?" Jim breathed the air deeply into his chest, letting out small waves of tenderness over the freshly-washed sidewalks.

"This reminds me of a painter from Romania," said Fred in low voice. "She was so narcissistic that on her good days she wondered how the rest of humanity could live without knowing her. She emigrated to New York where nobody knew her. She died last year, forgotten by all."

"Yes, what I like most over here is that you don't exist," Jim continued his frenzy. "You can walk naked in the streets or die right here in front of St. Patrick's, and no one will notice you, no one will see you. No one would look you in the eye, not even by mistake. They run around madly, like wound up toys, their cell phones hanging by their ears; they swarm, programmed toward exact targets. Eh," Jim softened his voice, "but the magic of this place saves both them and us."

"Which 'us?'" Fred felt himself under attack again. "Which us?"

"I mean us, artists…" said Jim swiftly.

"I don't know. I've become paranoid and suspicious. Us, people with migraines. Us, with our lost dreams… I have the feeling that I'm being betrayed by words—I, who was both a words' master and their faithful slave. I no longer have control over them, I no longer master their meanings, their heaviness, their symbols, which I once played with and turned over at my leisure. I don't know how to put it. I feel like a stranger. Not in this city, but in my own skin. You were talking about another planet? I think I'm from there, too. My body takes on a shape that I don't recognize. I look at my hands, and they're not mine. More and more often, I dream of myself swimming in a void, in waterless lakes; I want to run away, but my legs won't listen to me. I'm voiceless. I feel a great helplessness come over me. I keep on thinking: what can really save us in the end?"

Jim was silent for a while, taken aback by his friend's confession. He glanced at Fred's face which wasn't showing any pain and swiftly recovered. He, too, had these moods sometimes. The separation from the body. Beautiful. The body lags behind. It's normal. We don't recognize it anymore; we almost don't need it anymore. What are we? Temporary carriers of recycled energy. We accumulate experience through our own sacrifices. If only something came of it all, if this inheritance were of use to someone, somehow, God knows when. Where do our years go? Does anybody get to live them again, or do they simply get lost without a trace after they've sucked all our sap out of us?

An ambulance siren drowned the street's bustle for a couple of seconds. Fred's face narrowed in pain. He couldn't stand loud noises. He thought his cell phone was ringing. He fumbled through all his pockets with trembling hands. He found it, grabbed it, checked the screen. Nobody had called.

They arrived at Barnes and Noble, and Jim wanted to please him, knowing Fred was a lover of bookstores. The abundance of colors and the commercial designs of the books' covers bored Jim, and he wasn't particularly interested in their content, so whenever they went into a bookstore, he'd get a cup of coffee and leaf through an album with Munch's paintings while waiting for Fred to finish enjoying the place. Fred put on his glasses, and his face took on a sensuous expression. He stared avidly at each book that he took in his hands and felt as if he wanted to devour it. He could have done this for hours. Usually, Jim had to take him out by force.

Surprisingly, Fred didn't want to go into the bookstore this time. Harry Potter volumes crammed the shelves. Some of them were luxurious, hard-covered with golden letters; others were smaller paperbacks with a DVD or the author's photocopied signature; yet others were unsigned but had the Map of Miracles. The store's doors had opened at midnight, but a line had formed the previous afternoon. Over a million copies sold in the first few hours.

There was an endless queue at the check-out. The Easter holiday was drawing close; with the latest volume in the Potter series just coming out, you couldn't imagine a better gift. Fred pressed his forehead to stop the gushing of words that struggled to come out, and then felt his heart. Jim glanced toward him calmly. Fred took his cell phone from his chest pocket. He only thought it was ringing. It wasn't.

They stayed in front of the windows for some time, but Fred stubbornly refused to go in.

"I don't feel like it. This abundance of titles tires me."

"It does? Since when?" Jim wondered frankly, but Fred no longer heard him.

He remembered the launching of his novel in Bucharest, published before the revolution, when he was still read and celebrated. The bookstore was totally full, friends, writers, artists, students on their tiptoes to see him at the desk where he was giving autographs under the reporters' flashes. His mother was in a corner in her elegant suit, the color of baked grain, receiving congratulations, her demeanor proud and restrained. He was wearing a blue shirt that emphasized the brightness of his eyes and his tan skin with an, apparently negligently, knotted handkerchief. He shook hands, kissing, embracing, smiling self-assuredly before the cameras and the reporters waiting in line to interview the author. Then there was a party at Athene Palace Restaurant where he'd squander all the money he made on the book.

In comparison, the launch of his last novel, blacklisted by the censor and published after the revolution, seemed more of a vigil than a celebration. Few people, quiet, glancing at him coldly. No youngsters in the bookstore. Some former classmates, some writers and magazine editors who didn't know how to approach him. Fred had felt more of a stranger in the city of his birth than in New York. His mother had fallen asleep in the front row, her mind elsewhere. A slippery or perhaps stiff world that no longer had an appetite for others' celebrations, each preoccupied with his own survival.

The successful author of the Potter series that had ravished the New World smiled broadly in a poster the size of an apartment building, and in a smaller sign, the boy who'd played Harry Potter in the movie series had disheveled hair and an irresistible squint beneath his round glasses. Jim beamed.

"Quite a book!"

"What book?" Fred broke out, feeling the unease of his veins in his forehead about to dilate.

"I haven't missed a single volume. I'm crazy about it."

"Children's literature."

"Don't judge me by my age. Years passed over me, but I don't feel them." Jim breathed in deeply, with a silent, satisfied thought that he'd saved his childhood on time. "Who could have thought that this blonde would become richer than the queen of England? But she writes beautifully, you know, despite the fact that she's successful," Jim insisted, without realizing that he was pulling Fred through mined territory.

"Books, like people, have their destiny," Fred found himself explaining, as if he were sitting in front of Dr. Rohmer. "Some are simply lucky. With good timing and a generous promotion, a well-written book can be transformed overnight into a best-seller. People take what sells for granted. You tell them it's a masterpiece and they'll see it as a masterpiece. People here aren't alert; they trust authority. And they're perfectly manipulated by mass media. Quiet and obedient. Commercials work like a virus. We were suspicious in Communist Romania; we detected, but tried to ignore any form of propaganda to stay sane. Here propaganda, it's called promotion, the difference being that it doesn't target the political, but relies on the commercial spheres. One censorship replaced by another. But how can you read this childish stuff?" Fred didn't give in, though the noises in his head were roaring louder and louder.

"We love fairy tales, Fred," Jim suddenly felt himself a part of the great national choir. "We hope for miracles; we think dreams should come true. For me, a good book is one that puts me in the best world. And this one really is very well written, you know. I can totally identify with tiny Harry."

"Good for you. You're sounding like Mimi."

"Well, your Mimi understands something of this country."

"Indeed! She could even give lessons."

"At least she lives in the present," replied Jim.

"You have no idea what relationship she has to the future! Mimi usually lives all over the place, and more than once. A light shining on her would show seven shadows, not just one! Myself, I am not sure I even have my own shadow left."

"Man, you know what your problem is? You take things too seriously. I've seen this with other immigrants from Eastern Europe, too. You're too deep into the meaning of humanity, too intense, too—how should I put it?—too profound. We need simple stories here, through which to confirm our existence, not provoke or contradict it. Metaphors, metaphysics… No one has time for these things; no one gives a damn about them."

Jim's words took Fred back 20 years to Romania under the dictatorship that still haunted him.

"You're good, *mon cher*," a courtly poet had told him then. A poet who managed to get invited to parties with artists and writers, although suspected to be an informant given his frequent travels to the West. His work was always present in the volumes of corrupt homages published each year on Ceaușescu's birthday. "Your novel would become a best-seller if it got translated and published abroad. Have you ever thought of this?"

"I don't have utopian thoughts."

Fred had stroked his beard, unhappily, convinced that this was a provocation meant to pump him dry. The displeasure of having to deal with the censorship had been enough for him; he didn't want any other political complications.

"Had this been a normal world, your book would get translated and pushed in the West. It would make waves, trust me," the poet had gone on. "What does success mean here? Small culture, well-hidden country, closed society, out there they don't even know we exist. We float like pieces of paper in a kettle. Wouldn't you be interested in real competition? To go head to head against the really big writers? See, we compare ourselves among ourselves and it turns out that Popescu is better than Ionescu. The competition lies elsewhere."

"Perhaps it's elsewhere, but surely not where you think," Fred had said, looking at him more carefully for the first time. "I feel good in my own skin."

"Talent comes with a duty," the same poet had tried him, maintaining an ironic smile.

"And what would that be?"

"To become well known abroad, famous, and to pull the culture you come from with you."

"Do you see me as an engine of Romanian literature? Or are you pushing me to defect?" Fred had smiled, lighting up his pipe with a confident though nervous hand.

"God forbid! I push you to be a leader. To want more than this half-assed success."

"We're talking about a European country, though."

"Without an echo," the poet had answered drily. "Rather than make waves in an aquarium, it is better to test your skills in the ocean."

Fred had stared him straight in the eye. Was he honest, or was he merely an experienced diversionist?

Some years later, that same poet would become in charge of political censorship, a high position in the Central Committee of the Communist Party. Fred had just finished another novel that had been banned on the pretext that it was "intellectualist," that its characters were negative and the collective atmosphere depressing, in flagrant contrast to socialist triumphalism. For weeks Fred had to negotiate with the censor who always asked him to change or take something out of his book.

"I can't accept publishing a butchered book. Better to let it go," Fred had said stubbornly.

The censors breathed a sigh of relief, except Fred threatened that he would alert Radio Free Europe and would find a way to send his manuscript abroad. The old courtly poet, now the censor in chief, didn't hesitate to present a different argument this time.

"I don't know how much your books would have sold abroad."

"I thought you were saying, not long ago, that I deserve to be translated, promoted, known outside…"

"Because I had expected that you'd eventually learn the formula for success, that you'd understand the struggle to reach universal meaning. Stop writing about the political context here. It's unprofitable, and, what's more, is provincial to remain stuck in national obsessions. Believe me: no one cares how and in what way we live here."

"I didn't meet your expectations, in other words; you bet on me as on a horse that eats fire and flies over seas and countries, while all I do is foolishly feed on dry stubble."

The censor had not argued with him, and continued to recite his lesson unruffled.

"Listen, our readers are used to reading between the lines, waiting for allusions and political ironies that give them the illusion of rebelliousness. They read either for art's sake, or to calm themselves down from a futile, silent fight against the system. In the West, none of these formulas is valid. There, you have to tell them straight and fair only what they are prepared to hear. Do you think you're ready for that?"

"How do you know what's going on over there so well?"

"I need to; it's what I do. And I've travelled, I've opened my eyes, I was curious to see how life is elsewhere. Do you think your books would be successful if we didn't live in a dictatorship?"

"What do you mean?"

"If the system you criticize falls, would your books become dated? No one would care about them and no one would read you anymore. You're very lucky we have the dictatorship. People think you're courageous, but you've actually built your fame on our government's back."

"It's obvious you've understood little." Fred had held his own, although he'd felt like leaving and slamming the door behind him. "A writer forms his public; he doesn't take it for granted. In our closed society, the writer is more than a story-teller, he also plays the role of historian, psychologist, sociologist…"

"And you were saying you don't have utopian thoughts?" the poet had shaken his head, smiling ironically.

Fred had learned the rule from the censors: what mattered was who was the first to give up. And his only chance was to keep his answers short, to avoid getting nervous or making some scandalous declaration—not to enter into a dispute about the subject at hand or lose his temper and give up on publishing his book.

"What are you trying to say?" Fred had a comeback while the chief censor lowered his voice compassionately.

"We'll publish your book. Anyway, it won't change anything or anyone. Another bottle thrown into the ocean. But I don't suggest you jump into that other ocean. It might swallow you up."

Men and young women, children and grandmothers were coming out of the bookstore carrying *Harry Potter* in bags especially printed with the hero's figure flying through a window toward the sky. The shoppers' eyes sparkled with joy.

"Let's leave. This circus is making me sick," Fred heard himself saying.

"I know what your problem is," Jim softened. "You feel like a worker fired from a Ford factory when he sees a Ford roaring down the road. Or one at an arms factory, let go after the end of the Cold War, when a colder war is happening now. But you should know that you have nothing to do with their failure; it's not your fault that the world is moving in the wrong direction."

Fred's face reddened in aggravation. He stared at Jim as if he were an alien suddenly fallen from the sky. As Fred sought words, he couldn't free them from the box where he had lately kept them locked away, afraid they might reveal him.

"Do I look as if I need comforting?" he murmured.

His eyes had begun to tear, perhaps from the wind that had just strengthened.

"What? My goodness! Have you lost your sense of humor?" Jim lowered his voice to those tender inflexions that he had long gotten unused to. "Forget all this nonsense and let's go eat somewhere."

They went across Rockefeller Plaza Promenade where thousands of daffodils and yellow tulips seem to have been planted overnight among white blooming lilac trees. Fred stopped, trying to light his pipe. The headache pulsed against his temples. Jim pulled over to the side to wait for him, staring lackadaisically at a group of blonde women in jeans; they laughed, most probably about nothing. Fred saw them as well and let his eyes linger, over their faces, while trying his lighter dozens of times until he finally succeeded in lighting his pipe. The spring wind stopped, or his hand was now steady.

The women roared with laughter; they were out and were having *fun*. The magical American word. The meaning of life. *To have fun*. One of them looked strikingly like the young Mimi.

Mimi's obsession was also to laugh as much as possible, as often as possible; she'd learned all the rules of this New World. She was crazy about having fun, chasing a poster of happiness and getting ready for never-ending youth. She liked jokes and jests, superficial society where all show off their teeth and ask each other exasperatedly how they're doing, only to have a chance to answer that they're doing great.

Mimi had different levels of laughter, from a slight smile—complacency—used especially with her American business partners, to the uninhibited rough roar of laughter, which came out when she was with her

Romanian entourage where she loved to hear jokes—the dirtier, the better. She would then produce unpleasant sounds, her face contorted and her head thrown back.

It matters how a woman laughs when she lets go; it says a lot, not just about her level of education, but about her behavior in bed. Those that roar are hard to satisfy.

"How about a cup of coffee, baby? I know a cool place," Jim tried to start a conversation with one of the blondes. But the flock grew silent, cautiously walked away from him to mix in with the crowd.

His long hair tied in a ponytail, his red, unkempt, drifting Viking's beard, his wrinkled face and his eyes with dark circles, the brown lipoma on his right cheek that he had never bothered to get rid of, the vest with opened buttons and his pants soiled by paint might as well have belonged to a madman as to an artist. Jim grinned in disappointment.

"I'm telling you, we're going down the drain. These chicks don't know about attraction, about flirting, about elegance or fore playing. They want to go straight to bed, and if it doesn't work out, they pretend to make-out with each other or run to the therapist. I foresee the dissolution of the sexes," Jim shook his head affectedly. "Stress. And pollution. They were saying on TV that because of pollution, male frogs are about to disappear. Only female frogs are being born. They'll invade the Earth. We've become the weaker sex; we're feeble and we're not doing anything to defend ourselves. We're allowing ourselves to grow fearful, like fools. We're heading toward another matriarchy, this time around insatiable and loud."

Rockefeller Plaza was full of tourists who took pictures, sat on benches, ate sandwiches and rested their legs, swung around here and there by a sweeper who gathered the cigarette butts pedantically into a long-handled dustpan.

Fred had finally lit his pipe, sat down on a bench and noted something in his blue notebook. When he looked up, he noticed that a short man with a mustache had pointed his camera toward him. He went numb for a moment. The man pushed the button, and Fred had enough presence of mind to partially cover his face with his hands. The hammers kept beating in his temples with dizzying speed. He jumped up and hid behind some lilac bushes that surrounded the water fountains in the middle of the concourse. The man with the mustache had moved over to the side to keep him in focus and shot another photo. The flash caught Fred's open eyes this time. Terror contracted his muscles. He didn't even feel Jim's hand on his shoulder.

"What's the matter with you? What are you doing here? Hey, what's wrong with you?"

Fred made a sign for him to be quiet.

"He's photographing me."

"Who?"

Fred gestured with his head toward the man with the mustache.

"Who is he? Do you know him?"

"How should I know him?"

"OK, and so what? A few minutes ago we were singing praises to being just someone in a crowd, anonymous, and now this! Perhaps you've become a celebrity, and I don't even know it!" said Jim amused.

"Be quiet already!"

"Are you sure he's photographing you?"

Jim became circumspect and walked in the direction of the guy, who pretended to take pictures of the artificial skating rink and the golden statue behind it.

"Stay here, don't move," Fred implored him.

His pipe fell out of his mouth and into a row of daffodils. He stooped to get it and squatted without losing sight of the camera that clicked non-stop. Two Japanese women also wanted to take pictures of themselves with the water fountains and the lilac bushes and were waiting impatiently for Fred to get out of their way.

"I'll explain some other time."

"Tell me now. What is all this?" Jim became serious again. "Otherwise I'll go to him, yank the camera from his hands and stomp on it—for real. After September 11th, I could even shit right on him. *If you see something, say something.*"

"Mimi is having problems with her business. The IRS folks are after her," Fred gave up, knowing Jim's impulsivity, which had often gotten them in trouble.

"And what does that have to do with you?"

"They watch everything."

"Really?"

"I've been followed for quite a while."

"For God's sake!" Jim didn't give up. "How can they follow you? What's all this about? I'm going to confront him."

"Calm the hell down," Fred groaned.

But Jim got closer and looked the man with the mustache up and down. The guy kept his back to them and was now taking photos of the top of Rockefeller Center. He evaluated things coldly and relaxed, putting on his usual grin again.

"Come on, let's be serious. From the looks of it, this guy is a tourist amazed by his surroundings. He's got nothing to do with you, believe me. Look at him. He's taking random pictures. It's his first time in New York and he's overwhelmed, that's all. Let's get out of here so we can let these geishas gather memories. I've heard that this is how Asians have built their empire. They pretended to send us tourists and have scattered their spies all around the world. They take pictures of everything, go back home and copy us."

"You don't understand."

Fred grew irritated. But he did come out of his hiding place, raised his collar and started swiftly toward Fifth Avenue without looking back. Jim followed him, annoyed and uncomfortable.

"It only seemed that way to you," Jim said, "cross my heart."

"I think I have to go back. Mimi is expecting a FedEx and I promised her I'd be home after lunch."

"Let's grab some sushi, at least. I am so hungry I could eat a horse," Jim insisted, though he knew he'd reached a dead end.

"Not now. I have to go."

Fred left him in the middle of the street, crossed and slipped by the Sachs windows; he disappeared before Jim could get to shout that the man with the mustache had, just by chance, started in the same direction.

2.

FRED REACHED HOME LONG AFTER FEDEX
had left the packages for Mimi's salon with the porter. It
held large cans with mud from Techirghiol, a lake close
to the Black Sea considered to be miraculous after—
according to a legend—a scrawny donkey about to die
fell into the water and came out strong and healthy.
Wealthy New York women bought this miracle and had
mud treatments. Tiny Israeli boxes from the Dead Sea,
or creams with royal jelly and propolis that cost close to
nothing in Romania, but Mimi sold them in New York
with golden labels, along with the illusion of everlast-
ing youth to countless serious clients. More recently,
she started bringing over Gerovital, a medicine created
back during Ceaușescu's time by Ana Aslan, a genius
in geriatrics who had died long after she reached 90
years old, still looking good, and that fact helped sell
her product even more. Gerovital had long since swept
Europe by storm, and now Mimi had shipped it across
the ocean in the form of creams, ampoules, pills, gels
and powders, lining her pockets considerably. Manhattan was a paradise for those aspiring to immortality, a
product they bought with their eyes closed, willing to
try the most extravagant formulas.

Mimi had found a perfect niche. It's true that her conspiracy with fate had also worked. She'd learned the American word "opportunity," and she'd thoroughly searched for each and every one she could find. Americans are quite smart, she explained to Fred, because they exposed their children to positivism and self-confidence since early childhood.

"My love, it's obvious that a positive attitude attracts positive things. Why think of trouble before it comes? Instead you could use the power of your mind to attract good! Doubt may be something good in writing, for philosophers, I don't know, but the certainty that you'll make it can only be healthy when you have a purpose. And you also have to seize the moment, to know how to put yourself in the way of happy events." Mimi summarized her philosophy, putting on high heels and fussing in front of the mirror, imitating the gestures and positions of women that she had seen moving informally and confidently in the salon where she'd begun her ascension from a simple position as a receptionist to co-owner.

She learned to purse her lips when she spoke, controlled her strident laughter as much as she could and was careful not to move her arms around like a windmill. She straightened her back, heightened her neck by pushing her chin out, sucked her belly in and walked with her legs as close to each other as possible, studying her posture with sideways glances in the mirror.

From the same rich women whose behavior she had analyzed, she had also learned that the best reactions in any emotional environment are bored gestures, an indifferent glance, an expressionless face, and a sort of noble inattention—all without any commentary, exclamation or grimace. And Mimi was a diligent student, not without talent. In her adolescence in Romania, a gypsy woman had read her palm and told her that her ambition would compensate for understanding, especially in the second part of her life. Mimi believed in everything, but always kept a cool head on her shoulders.

She had become friends with Jessica, one of the beauticians at the salon, a girl who always seemed happy without a reason. She was unmarried and willing to socialize. Jessica was a chubby blonde slightly over 30, born in America to a family of Polish immigrants. She'd graduated from a Catholic school, then went to college to study social work, but she made more money at the beauty salon, where tips could be surprisingly large. In the summertime, she wore tight shorts on her chubby thighs, without any second thoughts, drank sugarless coffee but ate cookies by the handful. She had two rings pierced in her bellybutton, a brown hazel mole on her chin and washed-out yellow hair that she constantly pulled on and that shed everywhere.

Jessica had instinctively prolonged her adolescence to mask her immaturity. Her thoughts were always someplace else, oscillating between needlessly exultant moments to long periods of apathy when she locked through people and walked into objects. It was a sort of attention deficit disorder that many young people have. They don't pay attention to the outside world, not by lack of curiosity but because of a narcissism that will slow down with age. Or not.

Between the beauty sessions, Jessica had her earphones on and kept time with one leg, and then the other, as she ate hamburgers and fries from oily paper or devoured Chinese food with a plastic black fork from square containers. The smell of soy and ginger annoyed Mimi, still unused to Asian aromas; the smell of frying oil turned her stomach, but she was especially annoyed by the plastic fork that looked like a carbonized phalange. Mimi had been raised with traditional food served in porcelain dishes and savored leisurely at the table with real silverware.

Jessica had another annoying habit. She was joined at the hip to a bottle of plain water from which she drank every five minutes. By the end of the shift she'd finish about five of them.

"Why do you drink so much water?" Mimi had asked her, exasperated to see her with a plastic bottle raised to her lips all the time.

"We're told to hydrate."

"Fred says you, Americans, are the most naïve nation. You dress, eat and speak as you're told by people on TV and in commercials. And that is why you've become uniformed and so easy to manipulate. We did the opposite of what we were told back in communist times. We were taught to doubt everything."

Jessica stared at her with large gentle eyes.

"But it's good for you to drink water, you know. It's also good for your skin."

"When I was young, my mother used to tell me that frogs would grow in my belly if I drank too much water."

Jessica exploded in laughter and stared at her carefully.

"Is it true that in Transylvania they hammer a nail through dead people's hearts so they don't become vampires?"

"Where did you come up with that nonsense?"

"I saw a show on TV."

"God! Fred is right!"

Mimi told her about her childhood in Romania, her career as a ballerina in Paris, and about the book that Fred was writing, and after work Jessica showed her how to perform all sorts of facial treatments, relaxing massages and aromatherapy. Then they would go out to a bar, talk about nothing and laugh over glasses of colorful cocktails.

Jessica stared at the men grouped around beer bottles on the other side of the bar, almost all under 40 years old, wearing white shirts and loosened ties, loud, having come straight from work and hoping to spend at least one night with someone. Sometimes, Jessica went home with one of them, but a relationship had never come from any of it. Mimi stared at these men too and chose someone with whom she'd exchange glances all night, playing the game of seduction.

"I do it mostly to keep my figure, sex is just a sport for me. I don't care for any of them. Fred is more handsome and intelligent than all of them put together. And the most talented in the world. You should hear him speak!"

"How many years have you been married?"

"Three. But why haven't you gotten married? In Romania, girls your age can't wait to get married."

"And their careers? Anyway, I don't feel ready. I'm all right as I am. I even have a cat, have I told you?"

Mimi stared at her quietly, avoiding any comment, although she had this on the tip of her tongue: *what career?* This is why she couldn't marry? Or had she gotten used to things that way, to eating from a carton with plastic forks, to sucking from that water bottle all day and to running like crazy through the park on Sunday, because 'it is good for you to run too'? After she goes home she'll feed her cat and eat two huge cartons of ice cream—sugar free, of course—in front of the TV. If she waited longer, no one would marry her anyway.

Mimi once brought Jessica to Edi's apartment. They found Fred reading, laying on the living room couch. The girls giggled. Until Fred got wind of what was happening, Mimi was already in his arms kissing him, as always when she came home, while Jessica stopped by the door with a broad smile. From behind Mimi's locks, which covered her face, and from under her breasts, which she intentionally crushed against his chest, Fred measured Jessica and smiled fatherly at her, staring at her breasts already hanging down beneath her low-cut pullover and the brown hazel mole on her chin. Youth doesn't always help. He waved his hand awkwardly as to say "Welcome"—a show of pity—while Mimi was biting his right ear. Jessica's face turned red, spun around and disappeared into the kitchen, laughing nervously.

Mimi found her, eating a banana and bobbing her head.

"You Europeans are pretty perverse," joked Jessica playfully.

"Perverse?" Mimi stretched her neck playfully, ready to joke around. "Fred says that 'touch' has all but disappeared in America. *That's* perversity," Mimi pointed her nose higher. "And he says that, in the end, the invention of political correctness, good only up to a point, will fuck up your society—pardon my French. It sends chills down his spine. It reminds him of the ideological slogans he's run from. And what's so bad about touching in public if that's what you feel like doing?"

"Actually, couples intimidate me." Jessica avoided her question. "But he's so presentable and sexy! And he's also a writer, on top of it all. Very exciting! You're lucky, Mimi. And what does he write about?" Jessica pulled her hair, shedding long yellow hairs over cups and dishes, as she chewed her gum with that absentminded look incapable of focusing on beings or objects unless they were totally out of the ordinary.

Fred came into the kitchen, surprising them and offered them a glass of wine.

"Red or white?" Fred asked, looking at Jessica.

"Whichever is sweeter," she answered, pulling her bangs in all directions.

"Well, we have a problem. I don't think either one is sweet."

"Then red, chose Jessica," smiling and blushing again, while Fred took a bottle from the cabinet behind her, almost embracing.

"Narrow kitchens make things easier. They help bring things closer," Fred told her jokingly.

"Take the bottle and go to the living room. I'll bring some snacks in a second," ordered Mimi.

She placed the wine glasses in their hands and pushed the two of them out the door. They sat down on the couch. Fred turned on the TV, and while Jessica observed him with an admiring look, he gathered all the books, pens, glasses, some receipts, and carefully straightened all the tassels of Mimi's mother's tablecloth. He poured wine into the glasses; they toasted swiftly and stared at each other.

"How do you say *cheers* in Romanian?" Jessica wanted to know.

"*Noroc.*"

"*Noroc!*" Jessica opened her mouth to unveil her teeth and shook her blonde locks before sipping from wine that tasted quite sweet, in her opinion.

They were sitting close to each other. Jessica kept her knees raised, not at all comfortable in her short tight skirt that kept riding up her stout legs, to which Fred paid no attention. Instead, he started picking up the cat hairs from her low-cut pullover. It was just a reflex gesture, much as he carefully gathered the bread-crumbs from the tablecloth.

Jessica blushed even deeper; her acne inflamed and gleaming like rubies in lamplight. She stood quiet as his delicate fingers, barely touching her pullover, went on in their diligent quest for tiny, white hairs. She grew bold and took his hand and pressed it against her breasts, looking at the kitchen door from which Mimi might come in anytime. Fred quietly kept his palm on her chest for several seconds then gently took it away so as not to offend her, smiling innocently.

"Hairs annoy me. Is it Siamese?" he asked calmly, staring as a string of hair that he had just brushed off her pullover floated toward the floor.

"Yes, and she has blue eyes. Very beautiful. Like yours," Jessica answered him simply, and the redness on her face almost disappeared.

Mimi came in with a tray of sandwiches and seated herself on the couch, pushing Fred to sit in the middle. She crossed her perfect legs and raised her skirt to just below her panties.

"Ah, it's so warm! We can't control this device. In the winter it blows out too much heat, and in the summer you freeze. Why don't you take your pullover off?" she asked Jessica.

"I have nothing underneath."

"Do you want me to bring you a T-shirt or something?"

"No. I'm fine, thanks," Jessica smiled at her.

That's what she thinks, but it's not fine at all, thought Mimi. She already smells like an old maid. Perhaps that was because of the sweet perfume she used, mixed with the seborrhea and cat's smell, who probably slept in her bed.

Mimi owed Jessica a lot. First of all, because she had helped her enroll in a cosmetics course from which she'd obtain a certificate to practice after six months, but especially for what was to follow.

"My dear, I'll have a job from now on. And I feel that this will be more useful to me than my artistic record as a ballerina. You can see as well as I do that art doesn't really go far over here."

Fred breathed a sigh of relief. It was hard for him to tell her that in New York she had no chance as a ballerina and it had been impossible for him to suggest that she should do something else. To dance at her age was a bad dream. Luckily for Mimi, her practical side eclipsed her pride and saved her from impossible goals that would have only left her with frustration.

"My love, success has no smell. Am I right?"

"But I'm about to hear that it tastes quite good," Fred smiled ironically. Or bitterly.

"You always know what I want to say," Mimi softened her lips, feeling she was the center of attention. "And if it doesn't smell like anything, why should I care? I want to make it. That's all. It doesn't matter how or in what field. I'm ready!" she declared dramatically, then narrowed her eyes and rolling languorously, allowed her body to slip like a shawl down Fred's legs.

She unbuttoned his belt and lowered his zipper, staring at him provocatively. She caressed his member with one hand until it found its way out, and with the other she stroked herself over her silk panties. Fred raised her, twisted her, grabbed her cold buttocks with his palms. He bit the back of her head softly, knowing this excited her the most, and penetrated her from behind. Mimi's breasts grew, their hard, red nipples blooming like wild strawberries. He finished in her wet cunt that seemed eager to swallow him whole.

After they made love, Fred would have liked to hold her, to feel her hot skin and her swollen veins, to hear her swift blood settle back to its usual rhythm and flow; to absorb the trace of saliva that gathered at the edge of her mouth after each orgasm; to see a mere trace of the ecstasy that had just passed through her body. Most of all, he would have liked to see that something of himself had been impregnated under her skin, as the sign of a lost world could be incrusted in riverbeds.

After she climaxed with sharp and precipitated screams, as if she had just won a battle, Mimi immediately regained her usual voice, and became busy planning the next move on the chessboard, where she played by herself and was always triumphant. She'd resume her vigorous tonus and was ready to jump out of bed and pick up from where she'd left off. No trace. Fred remained in bed with his eyes closed, savoring the illusion of a new conquest. He felt fatigue envelop him gently, like a lazy waterway from whence a new, unnamed energy was bred, flowering in his muscles and sweeping his thoughts off.

Mimi appeared by the bathroom door, dressed, fully made up and seemingly untouched. And she was always ready to take it from the top again. The image of a huge piece of bread whose crumbs ants endlessly tear at came to Fred's mind. A bread that assumed his own form and dimensions.

He'd started exploring the city. During the day, when Mimi was working, he'd wander through libraries and museums, drink coffee in the East Village, read on a bench in Central Park while eating a sandwich, or, when the weather was bad, have lunch in the interior garden of the Frick Collection. He took in the bustling streets. He had his own places and habits: the bench in Gramercy Park where he had written a story in his notebook from start to finish; the table by the window of Dante Café; the narrow streets of Greenwich Village and the Tavola Calda Trattoria on Second Avenue, where a young waitress with ever-wet eyes would tell him in a musical English accent how she longed for her family in Sicily, a family she would never have left had poverty not sent her away.

Fred liked to talk with emigrants, and unlike in Paris, where they seemed prudent and grumpy, those in New York were open, always ready to tell their stories or share their hopes of making it someday, displaying an optimism taken over from the locals, perhaps from the subconscious need to affirm the solidity of their dreams in the eyes and reactions of strangers.

Fred caught the bug quickly and became excited with ideas and hope. Mimi was right. There was a good energy in New York; he sank deeper by the day into the depths of the city where he did not feel like a stranger. Manhattan slowly glued itself to his soul with its dimensionless space, despite the forest of skyscrapers that obliterated the sky. He was feeling good, even though no one knew him, though he had and knew nothing and felt like a newborn who could choose to walk down any path.

He had then begun searching for old acquaintances and friends from Romania who had moved to New York before him. First on his list, Anita, a much older painter, who lived alone in Forest Hills, preserved in cigarette smoke and the mist of alcohol. She'd once been a celebrity of Bucharest bohemianism, insatiably alive and with a sharp sense of humor that would hurt you at any point if you didn't meet her alert and malicious intelligence head-on.

Anita awaited him lying flirtatiously on the couch, wrapped in a blue Kashmir shawl that disguised her body deformed by age and abuse. But the shawl gave her green eyes the devilish brightness that dozens of men had rightly loved.

He rang her doorbell and heard only her tobacco-laden cough followed by a honeyed purr: "Come in!"

She didn't open the door or embrace him. Fred went in. He held a bottle of Scotch in one hand, and in the other a bouquet of flowers that Anita overlooked.

"Put the bottle down here on the table and let me take a look at you."

He agreed. He knew her moods and let Anita measure him, tapping a cigarette against a coffee table with piles of drawings, albums and books. She parted her thin hair with her skeletal hand—thin, but still long—freshly washed in his honor, and she glanced over at a seat placed strategically in front of her. She studied him in silence, like a piece in a museum that, no matter how much she liked, she wouldn't buy; then she laid back lazily on the couch and said to him:

"You're just as handsome! Too bad I didn't meet you at the right moment. I no longer have time to fall in love. And if I'm not in love, I couldn't care less about men. I can flirt intellectually, but that quickly bores me. Eh, tell me what's going on in Romania. Or better yet, tell me what's happening in Paris. Why did you leave? When did you get here?"

But she wasn't eager to find out. She sipped her Scotch and took in Fred with her eyes with the smile of the witch from Hansel and Gretel, as Mimi would have put it.

"Hey, if I were 60 again…" Anita sighed and mouthed the rest of her words with a dry cough. "All I can do is correct reality with the tip of the paintbrush."

One of Anita's works was on an easel at the other end of the spacious room—the portrait of a millipede woman with a unicorn head. Hands jutted out of her body, and each of them caressed the shadow of a man projected on the wall and floor.

"Beautiful work," said Fred. "These shadows are stronger than the bodies. Perhaps it's why I'm drawn to it."

"Hmm…" Anita moved moodily. "Perhaps. But I'm interested in the body, not in shadows. I stayed away from every spiritualist movement that appealed so much to rebellious folks in Bucharest. Transcendentalists, Esoterics, Onirics and whatever else they were. I cared about making art, not politics. True: I did have works that conveyed messages. Yes, I had wanderings, so to speak. But calculated wanderings. Well, such were the times. I had to give something in return. I had certain perks, right? Some accuse me of opportunism. I'd call it the capacity to adapt to a façade without selling your soul to the devil. And if I were to think in retrospect, they were fundamentally good works. In the end, history swallows and chews everything. What's left?"

"These leveling perspectives are dangerous," Fred heard himself saying.

But he didn't want to continue this dialogue, which made him feel worse and worse, poking at some of the wounds that had stayed unhealed, or at least unsolved, before now.

Some, like Anita, had gone through communism like a goose through water. They hid behind their art, which took the shape of the bowl into which it had been poured. But perhaps she was right. In the end, time is the only winner. What's left?

"My dear, believe me. Among all the dangers through which we move, history's just a farce."

"If it doesn't affect us directly."

"Then don't put yourself in its path."

"I can't go with the flow or lean into the wind."

"Beautiful. But damaging. Although I see that you've done pretty well for yourself till now," she said ironically. "You come from Paris to New York. Not bad at all."

"Can I light my pipe?"

"You can light anything you want."

She smiled insinuatingly. Fred wasn't in the mood for jokes anymore.

"You're too sensitive." Anita moved graciously toward the glass of Scotch, filled it up again and stared him straight in the eye. "Why do you complain? You're in New York. In Romania it's a mess."

Fred ignored her bitterness. It was better to turn the conversation toward Anita's turf, uneven as it was.

"I would have liked to know that you've remained a Romantic in your soul, with a foot in surrealism," said Fred, avoiding her glance.

He always said something other than what he would really have wanted to say, and this gave him an uncomfortable sense of guilt. This visit was his doing, so now he had to make the most of it.

"Ah, so you remember this…"

Anita relaxed and smiled, flattered. It was a comment made some time ago by an art critic in Bucharest that Fred had quoted to please her.

"Romantic? Yes, I was. I had good years. And enjoyable. Perhaps I would have created more if I hadn't yielded so much to pleasure."

"And how is it for you here?" Fred wanted to know, hoping that she, too, would return the question.

He lit his pipe again. He wasn't at ease. He felt Anita removed and strange, comfortable in her own skin, certainly in a well-defined, comfortable place. And this put him off more than the fact that she had mystified her biography under the pretense that she had been direct, honest and unforgiving with herself.

"I got here too late. I no longer have the strength to keep up with this stunning city. But luck hasn't left me. I have a sponsor, a couple of regular buyers. I'm old, sick, ugly and poor, but I don't complain."

Anita threw him a quick glance, waving to stop him in mid-air just as he was getting ready to contradict her.

"As you know, or maybe you don't know, I never wanted to leave Romania. I was spoiled there; why leave? I came here on a Fulbright. Despite Ceaușescu, one could still travel here and there on a grant. Here it so happened they liked me, liked what I was doing. They bought my paintings, gave me awards. I had exhibitions and got recognition. What to do? I stayed. But I don't consider myself an exile. I carry my home with me. I could live in a tent or on an island. Even in a coffin. I feel good wherever I go."

Anita widened her eyes, as if she longed to swallow him up. She'd remained the same, a capricious woman, used to choosing and playing, egocentric, untroubled by historical or personal dramas. Four of her husbands had died and several of her friends perished in communist prisons, but she kept on seeing to her work, painting, drinking and taking her afternoon naps, forever wondering how people, whom she thought the measure of all things, could allow fate to overwhelm them.

"It would have been easy in the old days as a decadent artist to become a drinker of cheap alcohol. I escaped thanks to my communist ideas, which seemed to me more humane and altruistic, and which protected me from the dangers of selfishness."

Fred was content to smile. Narcissists always think they're altruists. There was no point to getting into an argument. He was already tired; Anita had drained him of all his energy. He had come to listen, not to talk; to learn whether there was anything to learn, to test the waters through the eyes of someone who seemed to know where she was and had taken advantage of every turn of events, as she had done in Romania in the old days. He put his pipe back in his pocket and sought the door with his eyes to make sure he had someplace to run.

And yet he couldn't help but say:

"I didn't think that communist ideas could save anything."

Anita ignored his words. She seemed powerful enough to maintain her serenity.

"Yes, I humbly confess that they made me generous. And here, not at all paradoxically as you might think, I feel far more protected with my communist ideas than in Romania, where everyone confuses Ceaușescu's odious dictatorship with the utopia I fed on in my youth. I didn't change my hairstyle, although other emigrants from the East did. They simply changed their biographies to look like they were angels and dissidents; but no one flapped his wings under the dictatorship there, no one brewed any storms. I don't care for them all. I stayed the same. They might as well crucify me!"

Fred glanced at her with a cold eye, just how he'd look at a surreal painting where he couldn't spot a single brushstroke of Romanticism.

"And you?" Anita asked him, lighting another cigarette. "What do you hope for? Do you think you'll make your peace with being anonymous here, after everyone knew you in Romania? Because whatever you do and however you make it here, you'll still be a small voice in a big choir. We're talking about a continent, and not one particularly fond of the arts and literature. They don't even know their own writers. Check how many people have heard of Updike once you leave the narrow literary hallways. Not unless you hit the jackpot—excuse the cliché—and make money with your books. But since you say you don't go with the flow..."

"I don't see why I should make compromises to my freedom."

"What freedom? Just wait till you get an agent, and then an editor. They'll teach you how and what to write. You either adopt the formula for success that the market imposes or you go play at home with crayons."

"I don't think so," Fred said, "It can't be that way."

"You're funnier when you let your guard down and are naïve. It's exactly that way. Why don't you ask Sebastian? Look, he's a great example! One of our own who made it. And he's not all that talented, either. But he's shrewd. He knew how to do things. He whined to anyone everywhere that he'd been persecuted by the communists, by the Nazis, by fate, and lo and behold, his story touched them. They gave him awards before he could write a decent book. A dissident, this Seby, a holocaust survivor, the whole package. The more awards he wins, the more he whines."

"It's immoral."

"Hmm," Anita rolled her eyes. "Failure is immoral. Who's talking about morality? What kind of world do you think you've come to? Have you heard of opportunity? Eh, you're in the world of opportunists. Of people who hunt fortune down and who put their foot in the smallest door opening."

"Brodsky, Nabokov, Kundera were all emigrants, and they all made it."

"They have an abundance of talent. Don't misunderstand. You're talented—not like them, if you'll forgive me—you're talented, but you come from a minor culture, an uncirculated language. You need large props. Or large compromises. I won't give you lessons. I have a friend, a mediocre Russian writer, who, after some failures, published with a large press. He told me his formula for success: sex, crime, religion. There's this possibility, too, if political victimization doesn't suit you. You see, it's easier with painting. It's wordless. You like it, you buy it. You don't pay for the painting, but for the painter's name. I knew how to paint; all I had to do here was make a name for myself. But I'm not a good example; I was lucky. I found myself in the right place at the right time."

"Do you know Sebastian well? Could you put me in contact with him?" Fred struggled to ignore the self-confidence that Anita never shied away from showing.

"We don't see each other. There is not enough space for two of us in the same room."

"I only asked; otherwise, I don't think we are a good fit. For the time being, I want to finish my book. The publishing and promotion process has mattered too little for me until now. In Romania, it all happened by itself."

"Exactly."

"I believe in integrity. Maybe I'm old school."

"What can we do about it, darling?" Anita regained her superiority. "We are what we are. At the end of the day we're making waves, that's all. And we throw a pebble, now and again, into the ocean. I wish you all the best."

She lit another cigarette and fixed her eyes on the easel in front of the couch. She'd grown tired. She didn't show him to the door, but she followed him with a melancholy look, and it seemed to Fred that the devilish green reflexes in her eyes had softened into a strange gentleness, a sort of pity camouflaged as aloof sympathy.

He had come to see her thinking that she'd be able to help him somehow. She was a well-connected woman who moved in important artistic circles. A door slightly ajar would have been enough, but Anita only saw herself. Her portraits at various ages were hanging everywhere in the house. Since arriving in New York several months earlier, it was the first time that Fred truly understood that he'd have to swim by himself in an ocean where he was afraid to look back and could hardly glimpse ahead.

It had begun to snow outside. Christmas was closing in and the gardens in Forest Hills were decorated with colored lights. Skeletal deer sparkled by deformed dwarfs with green and red hats. But it was somber in the subway. Exhausted people slept with their chins on their chests. What was he really doing there? He felt no connection to those people who had seemed to bring all the sadness of the world with them, who emanated misery and the feeling that from there they'd have nowhere to run. It was the last stop for them, a sort of circle that closed and caught them inside.

He went across Manhattan underground, and it took him over an hour to get to Brooklyn, where in apartment windows, menorah candles flickered for

Hanukkah. Mimi's image moving in the warm kitchen, hugging him in the hallway with joyful cries—as if he'd just returned from a battle—was the only light for him during the holidays.

"How was your meeting with the witch?" inquired Mimi as soon as he got home.

"She's still the same corrupter of strong or drifting souls. She sits on a wax chair over the fire but she doesn't melt."

The description annoyed Mimi.

"What do you all see in her, for God's sake? She's just an egotistical hag who was a frivolous hussy in her younger days and ate three men for breakfast."

"But those men fought to be on her menu."

"Hmm…" Mimi placed her hands on her hips. "And how did you escape?"

"I was too unripe."

"And you say it just like that?" Mimi wondered in all frankness, widening her beautiful eyes.

Fred sensed her breasts stirring beneath her blouse. She stood in front of him with her legs slightly parted, her chin stretched out and her back straight, furious and provocative. Her upper lip trembled, and Fred struggled not to toss her right onto the bed. He raised the ante, calculating his moment.

"What attracted me to her was always one thing: talent."

"And this talent can excuse anything?"

"Sometimes, yes."

"I detest her."

She was irresistible with her mouth like a forsaken foal's. Her tense body radiated heat. Before Fred got to rip her panties off, Mimi managed to whistle between her teeth:

"She's just a perverted communist! I hope she'll burn in hell!"

They tumbled onto the carpet, their legs intertwining and tore off their clothes.

When she was very excited, Mimi's neck reddened and her voice thickened.

"Penetrate me now, take me now," she implored Fred hoarsely as her entire body trembled as if crossed by an electric current.

Suddenly, the bedroom door opened and Edi stormed in with disheveled hair and fogged glasses:

"Ceauşescu has fallen!"

Both stared at him as if he were a madman and remained on the carpet petrified. Edi glanced at them from above, struggling to ignore the situation. Seeing them upside down, naked and twisted between the bed and the desk, Edi had gained a certain authority, despite his frail body and having been taken by surprise.

"Come on already! It's all on TV! And I've brought you today's *New York Times*. On the front page: Revolution in Romania! What the hell, didn't you know anything about this?"

"How should we know?" Mimi raised her voice, annoyed that she hadn't climaxed.

Fred rushed to the living room and covered the TV with his sweating body; the lamplight projected a disproportionately large shadow on the wall. It had finally happened! He'd never thought this would happen in his lifetime.

When the Berlin Wall fell, he was in Paris, and for some time an enthusiasm that was more of an unrest haunted him. He had hoped that Romania would also be touched by the shockwave, though he feared that Ceaușescu's dictatorship would stand stone-still forever.

Despite everyone's prophecies and the tensions that seethed in Eastern Europe, the country had quietly gone on, and the oppressive system seemed more stable and sure of itself than ever. After all the other Eastern European countries freed themselves one by one, his enthusiasm melted away and he stopped following the inertia that festered in Romania. And look now: the "polenta had exploded" finally. And he wasn't there, just when he most desired to be there.

"Put something on," Edi shouted over his shoulder. "There are women around, too…"

And he pointed to Mimi. Fred stared at him sideways to see whether the Romanian Revolution had just magically awakened his sense of humor. But Edi's face became composed again.

Fred immediately reappeared with his shirt unbuttoned over the first pair of pants he came across, pulled quickly from the closet, and he sat himself in front of the television again, his heart about to leap out of his chest. His first reaction was not one of joy, but of indignation. He addressed Edi, just because he needed to talk to someone. Mimi remained hypnotized in the middle of the room.

"And these Americans, who for 25 years haven't said a word about the disaster Ceauşescu led that country into... Now they swoop like ravens over the corpse of communism; they only care about sensational news, without realizing that the real sensational news was the years of hunger, humiliation and isolationism. Nixon even invited Ceauşescu over; he took walks with his wife, and Ceauşescu shook hands with Mickey Mouse in Disney Land, while abandoned children in Romania were thrown into orphanages and miserable hospitals that looked more like extermination camps. We're talking about a European country, still, where a madman was allowed to do as he pleased. The queen of England took him on rides in her carriage, waving delicately to us beneath her pink hat."

"That's it! I need to leave now," announced Edi, putting his plaid scarf on over his grandfather's overcoat.

"Leave how? To where? Don't you want to stay and see what's happening?"

"You watch by yourselves. At 6:00 PM I have to be on 47th Street, you know that. Business doesn't stop for the Revolution in Romania. In the end, who cares?"

Fred glared at him. For the first time, he hated his own powerlessness. He should have done something and moved to his own apartment by now. What did Edi care? What did he know about Romania? He had left as a 13-year-old.

Images of a burning Bucharest continued to flow behind hasty announcements of broadcasters who mixed information at random—more or less real— about a country Americans knew little more than that it was Nadia Comaneci's birthplace.

Fred stared at the grandiose public spectacle, almost losing himself in the television screen. It was an indescribable mess, a mixture of fevered enthusiasm, uproar, and a joyful romp. Men carried small children on their shoulders; flowers were being thrown off balconies, women laughing hysterically, the elderly crying for joy. Everyone made the victory sign with their raised fingers, and danced in the streets, flowers fell from every window. Cars honked non-stop, flags waving from their windshields.

"It's like our national soccer team winning a championship!" Mimi said to him excitedly, seeking his eyes to read his reaction.

But Fred didn't seem to hear, and every comment irritated him. He would rather have been left alone right then. He felt as if a knife bore through him to his core. Each image on the screen opened another door that he had struggled to keep closed since he'd left Romania. On the main boulevard, tanks chock-full of occasional revolutionaries were waving flags with holes in the middle. The symbol of communism had been shot through. He thought he recognized Nick, a former classmate, waving a flag from a military truck. He moved closer to the TV. It was strange to see the city of his childhood and youth on American television, from somewhere in Brooklyn—and in such an explosive way! He wanted to run to the airport and return home on the first flight. Where was home? Had his mother taken to the streets to celebrate the victory, or better said, the overthrow? Whose overthrow? Ceaușescu's dictatorship? Communism's? For how long? After the fall of dictators, unrest or civil wars sometimes begin. What would happen over there?

In the background, he made out the rebuilt building of the former Scala apartment complex, which had collapsed during the big earthquake in 1977. Old memories came back to him. He felt a chill run down his spine. Dana's image lit up on the wall of the bakery where, on the evening of the fourth of March, they had left to buy her favorite sweets, amandines and eclairs. It was unusually hot for that time of the year, *a suspicious heat*, as his mother had said, leading him to the door after they had dined together in the old house in Cotroceni.

Fred was going to take her home, but first they took a walk. It was a full moon; the perfume of blooming hyacinths and daffodils enveloped the residential neighborhoods. The first crickets chirped, and once in a while they would stop to stare at the lit windows of wealthy homes with tall ceilings, baroque candelabrums and massive mahogany book shelves along the walls. The mystery of the lives behind the curtains attracted both of them. Sometimes through those windows they glimpsed a shadow moving, not knowing the figure was being spied on. This too added to their pleasure. From time to time they stopped, hugged and kissed, were happy and felt free despite the lock on freedom imposed by the regime. Youth is always stronger than time, he thought. They had bought the cakes, and the aromas of vanilla, chocolate and rum slipped from the paper bag.

"Ah, it smells so good," Dana had smiled, breathing deeply. "Like a fresh childhood."

"Why didn't we get savarins, too?" Fred spoiled himself. "I still like savarins most of all."

"Yes. Why not? Let's go back."

"Never mind!"

Fred pulled her against his chest, kissed her and held her tight for a couple of moments, careful not to crush the cakes that had filled the bag with steam from their heat. But Dana turned away and ran back to the bakery.

"Wait here. Don't move. Wait for me. I'll be right back."

He didn't move. He stood on the sidewalk smiling at her, looking at her long black hair as it bounced against her neck and her white giraffe-thin legs.

"I came out a giraffe, but I would have liked to have been a horse. Horses have something gentle and clumsy about them. They give an impression of freedom, but they don't know how to run too far... too far from their masters," Dana would say and slip into his arms.

After making love, they would glue their bare bodies to each other and press madly against one another until they felt their skin burn and her breasts melt into his chest. They pretend to "separate," promised to make love "desperately each time, as if it were the last time."

They had planned to marry in September. His mother had adored Dana.

"I couldn't wish for a better daughter-in-law. You're made for each other. I'll give her my grandmother's diamond ring as a wedding gift."

The ring would get to America eventually.

At first there was a rumbling. A sinister rumbling that was unlike anything else. It came from everywhere, from the ground and from the sky. One could hear the barking of dogs, taken out on walks, who tugged at their leashes as if they'd gone—and then a metallic trembling of windows, cracking as if the world had loosened into bits.

"Earthquake! Away from the buildings! Run! Run!" You could hear everywhere.

Then the true nightmare began.

People dashed up and down the streets. Some ran out of buildings, almost naked, and threw themselves, staggering, into cars' headlights. Windows burst and walls cracked. Roofs fell apart, cupolas, everything flew, rolled, crashed on the cement, spreading dust and fumes. Through windows one could see chandeliers thrashing from one wall to another, massive cupboards and bookcases falling. Fred had just started toward the door of the bakery to take Dana out when the noise reached a paroxysm. It sounded like the explosion of a huge heart. The old building with its many stories, apartments above and the ground-floor Scala bakery, tossed about violently several times and crashed in a compact cloud of debris. The lights went out, the earthquake stopped and for several seconds a deadly silence fell. Fred lay still, face down on the sidewalk, grasping the bag with its crushed sweets.

Two soldiers forced him out of the rubble after he'd spent hours desperately searching for Dana. He wobbled as if about to faint, his palms pulsing with blood and his eyes bloodshot. He had wept, vomited, and cried, putting aside bricks, beams, and pieces of wall and flesh, remnants of a crumbled universe where existences abruptly stopped in their most natural life situations.

He had found nothing, not even a shoe or a piece of Dana's soft thin blouse. As dawn approached, he fainted again. A stranger felt sorry for him and drove him home. He had barely succeeded in whispering his address before passing out. What point was there in taking him to the hospital? All the hospitals were crammed with seriously injured people and were too busy to care for a mere fainting spell. His mother was waiting, scared to death, by the window. When she opened the door, Fred collapsed on the threshold.

Toward the evening, when he got up to urinate, he noticed a strand of Dana's long hair stuck to his shirt, to the right of his heart, probably from when she had hugged him before returning to the bakery. He wept out loud again, holding the hair in his palm like a diamond bracelet, or a fragile bird whose pulse he still felt. He found an empty vial to put it in and felt as if he were saving a bit of Dana. He placed the vial on his nightstand, as some people kept an urn of ashes on a shelf. He would never part with that vial, Dana's sole surviving material essence.

For several weeks, he walked around like a robot, ate almost nothing, and laid in bed with the curtains drawn and the lights off, refusing to talk. One morning his mother came to the door, drew the curtains, stared at him for a long time and simply said:

"Life goes on."

And it did. But he never touched those kinds of sweets again, and the smell of vanilla continued to turn his stomach. Until, years later when he'd wait for Mimi in the evenings in front of the patisserie where she made crepes in a Paris neighborhood. The perception of the vanilla aroma metamorphosed slowly. Its hardness softened. It now had the taste of fresh wood mixed with strong French perfume that emanated from Mimi's hair and floated silently in the air.

Fred and Mimi had lived together for several months when, one night, Mimi told him carelessly as she put on her make-up before going out to the corner bistro:

"I cleaned up today. There's no space for anything in this small place. I threw out a bunch of silly things."

The vial had been thrown out, too, and Fred didn't protest. He felt nothing—only the flapping of a wing upon his heart and then a sense of liberation that replaced his sadness, as might happen if you threw a flower, to float on water in the memory of a dearly beloved and watched till it disappeared, swallowed by the waves, after which you'd breathe easily. He couldn't do anything else. Dana's image faded into spring, which had broken forth in Paris like a ship with swollen sails.

"Everything seems so easy now! Listen to what they say: the Ceauşescus have fled and the army, police, Securitate, everyone has switched to the revolutionaries' side without resisting in the least… You ask yourself, then, why the Romanian people didn't do it earlier, why they had to put up with it for so long if it was so simple?" Mimi addressed Edi, who was by the door, ready to leave.

Fred seemed far away, and Mimi left him to his thoughts, though she didn't like to feel her power evaporate together with this revolution, which in the beginning had enthused her, but now annoyed her. Edi shrugged his shoulders as if he didn't care.

"They did it when they were allowed to. I don't think any of this is by chance or sensational. A farce well played to leave the impression of a real revolution. In reality, it's just manipulation of the Western powers who signed a deal with the Russians."

Fred looked at him irritated, wondering why he didn't leave already.

"What do you mean to say?" Mimi rolled her eyes.

"The usual plot. Romania was the last country in Eastern Europe still holding onto communism. It was its turn now. Soon it will be over."

Following these prophetic words, Edi slipped out of the apartment and closed the door behind himself.

"An insufferable mannequin," Mimi murmured in Edi's wake.

She lay quietly on the couch by Fred. The news was interrupted by advertisements, and Mimi took advantage by trying to appease Fred, who seemed to have fled to a time she had no access to. She was jealous of his thoughts, his past without her, his present worries that excluded her entirely.

"Would you like me to make some coffee?" she asked him as gently as possible, letting her dressing gown open as if by chance, revealing her legs.

She hadn't had time to put her panties back on, and since Edi had left anyway, there was no point to bother.

"No. I think my blood pressure's high anyway. Come on, come here," Fred yielded and put his arm over her shoulders, pulling her closer to him on the couch.

"Then maybe… something else," Mimi purred, feeling that a small fissure had appeared in the wall Fred used to barricade himself behind, and through which he could have slipped again.

Counting on his carelessness, she placed one of her legs on his knees, and as the transmission of the Romanian Revolution continued to be interrupted by fast-food ads, which disgusted them both, she placed herself over him, unbuttoning the rest of her robe and blocking the TV with her body that was white as a lamp about to light up the whole city with all the tension she'd accumulated. Her hands moved swiftly, expertly, knowing what to press, what to caress, when to wait lazily for his member to swollen. She sucked his fingers one by one as she let herself be penetrated, cooing hoarsely in his ear:

"I don't like to leave things unfinished."

Then they heard the first shootings on the screen. Fred exploded inside her, and with a huge effort succeeded in lifting her so as to see how the revolution that had begun as "velvet" had transformed into a blood bath.

"God, what are they doing there? Are they shooting one another? Is this live?" Mimi cried, her eyes staring at the screen.

She jumped off the couch and put her hands on her head as she'd done in her youth, imitating her mother when she heard of some misfortune.

They showed images from Palace Square, bullets flying through the air, a melee, the crowds running beneath shooting firearms. There was a fire set to the National Library; shots were ringing out continuously, everywhere. On the balcony of the former Central Committee of the Communist Party, the revolutionaries cried into the microphones:

"No violence!" "Don't shoot!" "Stop the shooting!"

In the two days that followed, everyone had their eyes on Romania. The most contradictory news was issued from the TV screen: the Ceauşescus will be judged in an emergency trial; the bloody turn was due to the response of the guerilla troops faithful to the dictator that had tried to suppress the revolution, to liberate him and bring him back to power; the terrorists had poisoned the water, were shooting from atop buildings; they went into hospitals and slaughtered everyone they could, they were planning on blowing up public institutions, chemical plants, hospitals' blood banks. The broadcasters called on the people in the streets to oppose the resistance of counter-revolutionary forces. It was being announced that tens of thousands of victims existed throughout the country.

Mimi and Edi left for work in the morning and Fred stayed home, glued to the TV. He could understand absolutely nothing. Who was shooting whom? Why had everything begun like a joyful fiesta, and turned into a violent fight? Who was behind the bloody scene that had erupted as soon as everything seemed to be over? Perhaps people over there would be chased by terrorists for a long time, forced to hide; one nightmare would be replaced with another. Perhaps they'd live in an indefinite state of emergency, a continual civil war. And there was his mother, who was alone in Bucharest... What could he do?

He felt useless and ridiculous on his couch in Brooklyn, as useless and ridiculous as he had felt in the past during the years of obedience under the dictatorship. Things happened without him, outside of him; he was no more than a passive spectator of this dramatic overturning of communism which he had once hoped for in secret, but which he had given up considering.

He dozed off during the commercials on the news channels, tortured by questions, guilt-ridden by the heavy empire of fear, surrounded by newspapers, his telephone sitting on his chest. He had spoken several times with his mother, had called his family in Romania, as well as old friends and colleagues, but no one seemed to know or understand too much. Fear and confusion reigned over there, too.

Edi had his own theories.

"The secret service agencies are fighting amongst themselves. They need victims to legitimize this coup d'état. Who do you think the terrorists are? Special troops. Secret police, paratroopers, KGB, the dictator's snipers. They say Ceaușescu took orphans, raised them underground and trained them to protect him. The orphans had no mother, no father, no God. Ceaușescu and his wife were their mother and their father and their God. And Saddam's soldiers. The Arab terrorists had training camps in the Carpathians. Ceaușescu and Saddam were like brothers."

On Christmas Eve, announcements on TV said that the trial of the Ceaușescu couple would be broadcasted live. Mimi had made traditional *sarmale*—stuffed cabbage—and all three of them sat at the table in front of the TV. Edi didn't seem too happy. He didn't care for Mimi's Christmas, and the revolution had started to get harder and harder to digest. Mimi pushed:

"Do you think Fred could smoke his pipe in here?"

"Here where?"

"In the living room."

"No way."

"Oh, come on, not even during the revolution?"

"I don't want smoke in here."

"There's no smoke without a fire. And there is a lot of fire out there!" Mimi tried to be funny but Edi wasn't in the mood.

"Do you think they'll show us the trial?" Mimi kept on asking.

"God willing, all this stuff will end soon," grumbled Edi.

Fred jumped off the seat and turned the volume up. Sebastian Solomon himself was invited on the Larry King show, introduced as a dissident Romanian writer well-known in New York's literary circles.

"Do you know him?" Mimi asked, her eyes widening.

"Yes," evaded Fred, "though we were never close."

Solomon had a sporty red pullover on and narrated freely about Ceaușescu's tyranny, the starvation in the last years of the dictatorship, and political censorship. He gave juicy details about the dictator's habits with the cynical detachment of one who lived far from the nightmare but who could allow himself speculations that were convenient for the media, forever in search of the sensational.

"We lived in an absurd world. It's not surprising that the avant-garde and European surrealism had their roots in Romania," Sebastian said. "All you need is a Latin country and a dictatorship for the birth of the fantastic. Márquez proved it best."

Larry King was amused and promised to invite him on again.

"Look, this guy's become famous! Eh, eh, this is what I dream you'll become," Mimi said to Fred, unable to hide her disappointment that they still lived somewhere in Brooklyn at the mercy of Edi's moods—Edi, who valued nothing except for the diamonds on 47th Street, while others, perhaps less talented than Fred, had found a way to move forward and even became famous.

"Here, only actors and singers are famous," added Edi, but they both ignored him.

"Why did you never mention Solomon?" asked Mimi. "And if he's in New York, why don't you go see him? He seems pretty settled. And he's a good-looking man too."

"Your ideal guy, right?"

"My love, don't be mean," protested Mimi in a soft voice. "You'll surpass them all."

Edi looked at them knowingly and smiled as friendly as possible. Fred felt a cold chill run down his spine because he'd glimpsed a flicker of irony in his cousin's look.

Just as they finished the *sarmale*, which Mimi had made not with pork, as in her native country, but with turkey so Edi could eat it too, newscasters announced on TV that the dictator and his wife had been sentenced to death for sabotaging the national economy and for genocide. The simulacrum trial had gone by fast, in less than an hour. Then, two soldiers had raised the couple upright, the death verdict was read, their hands were tied behind their backs, and they'd been taken out to the yard of the military unit where they'd been prisoners.

They'd been taken to the wall where a makeshift platoon of soldiers had executed them. Everything had been recorded on video and soon everyone would be able to see it on their screens.

"They look like two wretched old folks," commented Mimi.

"Let's not get too sentimental. Scoundrels," answered Edi.

"But at least they show dignity," insisted Mimi.

"They're paranoid, not dignified. They can't believe they'll be killed. Can't you see? How could their beloved people do this?"

"I think Edi is right," murmured Fred. "They seem like frightened old folks who would come back with a vengeance if, by some miracle, they regained power. And their revenge would be terrible. It's quite odious; everyone will say we're barbarians, but I can't see any other solution than to kill them as soon as possible."

Ceauşescu had sung "The Internationale."

"What are you doing, children? I was like a mother to you," his wife had said to the young soldiers who were loading their guns with hate-filled grimaces and couldn't wait to shoot their dear "parents."

They didn't accept being blindfolded. The platoon almost couldn't wait to be given the order: "Fire!"

Immediately, dozens of bullets were discharged. Their bodies fell onto the cement, the blood flowing from their heads.

The images were sinister. Mimi felt nauseated. Fred seemed incapable of any reaction. He was ashamed, felt pity and horror and was at once obscenely gladdened and humiliated by the cruelty of the scenes they had just watched. He stood pinned to the chair, staring at the emptiness. History collects false heroes and crimes to justify its leap from one farce into another.

Many who had sung joyfully at the Ceauşescus' funeral would discover after a while that those who would take over would start to imitate the old oligarchs and be like them under the cover of wild capitalism in its first stages. The changes people had long waited for would take quite a while to make themselves felt, and the string of sacrificed generations wouldn't end just then. Only that they'd be too exhausted, too disgusted to start another revolution.

Even if Edi were right and the Revolution was staged—with the price of innocent victims—in the end it's the result that counts: communism had fallen. Yes, just like in a soccer game, what matters is the score, the final result. No one will remember how many players were fouled, eliminated, how many off-sides and misses…

Mimi stood by the door, undecided as to what mood to act out.

"Christmas meals are heavy," she whispered, observing Fred's frowning cold face. "Maybe you want to go out for a walk?"

"They shot the dictators. Now what? What more do you except? Everything will fizzle out a bit and then go back to normal. This is it, it's done, go to sleep," Edi told them and went to the bathroom with a grimace that could have meant anything.

Mimi cleaned up the table, and Fred went out to walk by himself. For the first time, he regretted that he had quit smoking; he needed something stronger than a pipe. The cold wind reddened his eyes even more. He felt suspended high up over a world that changed its relief, colors and sequences swiftly. What was he really doing there? He felt no connection to that place, the people that he saw going to or coming from work, always moving with a purpose, silent and serious, avoiding eye-contact and saying "sorry" whenever they'd touch one another by mistake.

He felt that life had stopped belonging to him. He was an open drawer on the street, and no one was curious to see what was inside. He lived a provisionary life in danger of becoming permanent with all his half-measures and half-finished projects. As if not being able to breathe in deeply. Going on tiptoe so as not to awaken inner voices that tell you that you don't own your own turf.

If during the two years spent in Paris he had known clearly that he was in exile, over in the U.S. he felt neither a foreigner nor at home. The terminal stop that Mimi spoke about didn't close off the road; it raised him above intersections from whence he could theoretically go in any direction. Only that the crazy traffic paralyzed one's movements, the noises covered one's desire, barely whispered from fear that in that crowd one could easily take the wrong path. What was the path? Once, it seemed to him that he could see it; now, he groped, caught in the wires that he himself had fashioned.

When he returned, Mimi had fallen asleep on his side of the bed, to feel him as he snuck in. Her bare shoulders, her hair scattered on the pillow, the acid smell of her breath might have been the certainty he needed. Would she agree to forget this road that didn't seem to go anywhere and go back to Romania with him? The dictatorship had fallen. They had a beautiful home over there, his mother, eager for him to return, friends, prestige, readers, a beautifully-paved way and an assured eternity. He would never write in English, anyhow.

To what end was all this useless strife; why should he confront his destiny, exchange peace and security for uncertainty and anxiety? He'd go back to a new country with a new aura after his sojourn in Paris and New York; he'd be more prolific and shine even more brightly than before. In essence, he was spoiled by fate; why should he dare to make it in New York? He could still stop the avalanche that had overwhelmed him and dragged him crazily downhill.

In Bucharest, a made bed and a ready table awaited him. Perhaps a few reporters would welcome him at the airport too. Mimi could open up a private ballet school. What if he woke Mimi and asked her right then?

The blinds were still raised and the fragile street-light trickled across the old desk, wrapped itself around the bedpost and stopped in Edi's outdated cupboard, where stacks of their things were piled, carried from one continent to another. The room seemed even smaller in the darkness, and felt colder. There was tightness in his heart: nothing was his. He couldn't even recognize his shadow backlit onto an alien wall.

Mimi felt his presence and turned her back like a child who had dreamed something unpleasant. For the first time, he looked at her with fear. Not even Mimi seemed really his anymore. He slipped beneath the covers and pushed her lightly, but it seemed as if she felt nothing. She was in a sound sleep, and he didn't dare disturb her.

Edi's words would soon come to prove providential. The following day, the American press turned toward a new conflict in Panama, and Romania became a lumbering democracy where the enthusiasm of the revolutionary days had been overcome by disappointment and revolt. Even Fred's mother spoke about crushed illusions and was happy that he was in New York, far from the frustration and deception that grew there by the day.

With the Romanian Revolution over and the holidays behind them, a stagnant sense of lassitude that became the norm, a feeling which always seemed to follow joyful or dramatic events, this time failed to discharge adrenaline and resulted in returning everyone to the monotony from before. Fred went back to his book, and Mimi continued her receptionist position at Fancy Soho salon.

Only, after several weeks, the owner of the salon, an Italian woman over 60, assembled all her employees during lunch to tell them that a month later she'd close the salon. She was selling her business because she'd met the man of her life, with whom she wanted to move to Tuscany, where her father had left her a vineyard at the foothills of Voltera.

Mimi would be without a job. She didn't want to abandon her cosmetics course, but it would cost much. There was no way Fred could work yet. The universities where he had applied for teaching jobs didn't seem to rush to answer him, and their savings were minimal. Edi had begun to show signs of fatigue after the prolonged three-way living arrangement had lingered longer than he liked.

Mimi tried to calm them, assuring both Fred and Edi that she would never give up, even if she had to work as a housekeeper for a while or care for elderly people at a retirement home. That's when Fred decided to seek out Sebastian Solomon. They'd both been part of a literary circle in Bucharest when Fred was very young and hadn't published a book yet. Sebastian—Seby, as he was called by those close to him—had encouraged Fred, by publishing two of his short stories in a Bucharest literary magazine that he was working on at the time, foreseeing a bright future in prose for him.

When he called, Seby seemed delighted. He knew something about Fred's evolution, had read one of his novels and was happy to find out that Fred had also followed the American path and was waiting to meet him readily.

Seby lived in an elegant apartment on Riverside Drive with a view of the river and park. He'd married an American woman from a wealthy family. Seby had become an emeritus professor at Columbia University and the head of the editorial board of an academic magazine.

Wearing light summer clothes and linen shoes with no socks, he hugged Fred with pretense affection and eyed him up and down for good measure, showing him the way to a huge room lined with paintings and books. He was probably fifteen years older than Fred, but time had been generous on him, worked with small measure and did not show its passing. Yes, Mimi had been right: Seby projected power and self-confidence, was accomplished and had made peace with his wealth.

The atmosphere was cordial, though artificial. Each faked interest in the other's life, but it was clear that their worlds would maintain their parallel distance despite the things they had in common. A shared natal country and language, exile and one's profession are not enough to join two people who happen to find themselves in the same room. Each of them quickly outlined his own personal inventory. Seby: two successful sons, a lawyer wife, ten published books and two vacation homes. Fred: had arrived too heavily clothed, and his forehead glistened in sweat.

They drank whiskey and spoke for a long time about the revolution. Seby seemed skeptical about the future, but happy that an American TV station would send him to Romania to file a report.

"A documentary that will probably wind up as a book. Only you know how it is, the book will sound more like what my editor will want than how I'd write it. At first, I was very conflicted, but then I understood that it's good to be on the practical side if I want to see my books out and a generous contract. You know how it is…"

Fred didn't know how it was, but he kept his questions to himself.

Seby gave him friendly advice, avoiding more intimate discussion and repeating: "You know how it is" more often, so as to impart a cavalier air to the discussion, or purely and simply because it was a verbal tic that he could not get rid of.

Fred ran away, thinking about how much loss of energy, how much every book published under communism took out of him, with the political censorship on his heels. Yet he had never sold himself out to the censors, taking the risk of not being published in the end.

"Why not go into a system that works instead of lamenting from the outside? After you answer the simple questions: What do I want to be, where do I want to go? It's good to study the rules of the world you've entered. A world built for champions. The mechanisms of success are set. But it's not all about accessing them; you also have to accept them afterward. You know how it is. The result is worth it even if you have to anesthetize your conscience. Are we talking about compromise? No, about adaptation. A-dap-ta-tion," Seby whispered bluntly, lowering his voice as if he'd just told him the greatest secret.

Fred was quiet, examining, by turns, the still-life painting of flowers above the fireplace positioned between two Lalique candlesticks, the stems of the tulips in the painting forming a fan in a long vase that matched the mahogany wood table perfectly, the soft Italian shoes and Seby's shirt sleeves, rolled-up with careful negligence, and the spines of books left at random by the edge of the couch.

"There's little understanding for failure here. Failures can be recycled at best, and only so that the loss on the part of those who invested in them won't be

complete. The losers are despised, in reality. Eliminated. You know the script," smiled Seby, winking at
him. "Actually, it's the same everywhere. Only here, we
pretend more and we also fake it a lot. Social welfare
programs, philanthropic foundations and the whole
necessary circus under the slogan: 'We care!' And I ask
you now: what's wrong with this political correctness?
I find that it's ordered society and sanitized it."

After which Seby excused himself, because his wife
had an appointment at a beauty salon, so he invited
Fred to a restaurant across the street.

They became even more estranged at the dinner
table. Seby was a regular at the place; waiters greeted
him with a mix of respect and warmth, a sign that
they'd all received good tips over time. His photos were
even on the back wall of the bar, alongside famous writers like Philip Roth and Saul Bellow. He seemed not
only adapted but in control in the new world that had
revealed its secrets to him on time and had opened up
a place for him at the table of the chosen.

Fred ordered fish upon Seby's recommendation; he
had guaranteed it would be the best grouper in a ten-
mile radius. They also drank two bottles of Sancerre,
but Fred kept quiet and watchful, rubbing his pipe in
his pocket now and again and discreetly stroking his
beard, which had begun to grow white. A sign of nobility, as Mimi would say.

"And let me give you another piece of advice,
though maybe I've spoken too much," Seby began.

"Keep away from the ethnic ghetto if you want to make it. And don't give up on the status of *foreigner*. In New York especially, it's a privilege if you know how to manipulate it. Exceptional foreigners are very valuable to the local milieu; they, Americans, suck their energy from them, for foreigners give power and vitality to this world. They even call them 'aliens with extraordinary abilities.' Don't be shy to immigrate as an alien with extraordinary qualities. Americanization is only for emigrants who have no other chance, neither in the country they come from nor here."

After dinner, they split as affectionately as they had met.

When she heard that he'd been at Sebastian Solomon's without her, without even telling her, Mimi had her first breakdown.

"What? Do you think I couldn't keep up with the conversation?"

"It wasn't a conversation, but a monologue," Fred replied, hoping that he'd end the discussion that way.

"Or maybe you're ashamed with me?"

"It's not about that. I wanted to surprise you…"

"You did!"

"I simply followed your advice. I had no desire to look for him."

"Fred, you know what? Till now things have gone like this: I took the backstage in our marriage of my own free will; I work so you can have time to write, to think, to reflect, to see people from whom you could learn something or get something from. I know my place, but don't brush me aside, do you understand? Don't treat me that way. Who do you think you are?"

Fred's face grew pale. Mimi had raised her voice, with thicker inflections. She spoke lowering her chin, her face had reddened and grown smaller from the aggravation. He had seen her that way once before in Paris, arguing with an emigrant who begged at the tables in the pastry shop where she made crepes. She'd gotten so excited that one could see her veins throbbing against her throat; the owner had to come and calm her down. For Fred, it had been an unpleasant and frightening show, which Mimi, tenacious as she was, realized she wouldn't perform again unless she wanted to lose him. But now that they were married and she found herself with a leg up on him, how much more should she take?

Fred went into the bathroom and locked the door behind him to avoid keeping the conversation alive.

"What are you doing?" cried Mimi, displeased that she hadn't finish up her side.

"I'm tired. I'm taking a shower."

"Take two!"

They slept with their backs to each other, each on his side of the bed. Mimi fell asleep at once, as people who have worked all day do, and Fred lay in the darkness seeking the strand of hair that he had let fall from his hand. But when?

Strained days followed. Fred could not write a word.

"Don't worry, my love, this is a sign that you've begun adapting to this world; don't they always talk about *writer's block* here?"

Mimi was increasingly agitated as the salon's closing day approached, and they communicated less and less with Edi due to his hostile attitude, which he had begun displaying at the thought that they'd live with him much longer than he'd anticipated.

But just when things seemed so bad, Mimi barged into the apartment one night loaded with bags, packages and flowers.

"Ta-daaa! Boys, God hasn't stopped loving me yet!"

They both stared at her like she was a comet that had fallen from the sky. Her eyes sparkled, her body trembled, and she radiated so much light that she could have lit up the entire neighborhood.

She let the door slam shut behind her and stopped at the living room, covering both of them with a triumphant, merry prankster's look. The intimidated Edi hurried to take her bags to the kitchen without anyone asking him. He saw her suddenly in a different light, for the first time observing her thin high waist, the naughtiness of her marble-like legs, her long arms that with every movement made her breasts jump under her rustling silk blouse. And that smell of green grass, of lemon peel, of wet skin drowned in flower petals, which he had never experienced before. A stunningly beautiful woman had lived in his home for a while. How had he not seen her until then? He felt the blood pulse within him. It emptied his head and turned his chest upside down. His knees cramped only to soften again in a moment, as if he'd just passed the finish line of a marathon.

Mimi set her moment well and gave them the news with a pirouette that almost made Edi faint. She'd received a part as an extra in a dance troupe at a theater on 42nd Street. Fred, who tried not to ruin her joy, embraced her, kissed her on her forehead and opened the champagne bottle that Mimi was already holding tight before her breasts.

They celebrated, ate goose liver with pickles and Manchurian caviar. Mimi dressed herself provocatively and put a pink goose feather in her hair. She got a bit tipsy and remembered jokes from Ceaușescu's time, and she laughed heartily, throwing her head back and moving her hands around. She told Edi that he'd be a handsome guy if he weren't so stiff and wore something other than the dark, shiny suit and his grandfather's overcoat. She forced him to drink strawberry champagne and sang the old popular Romanian song "Zaraza" to him.

Then she told them breathlessly about the audition, how she'd been chosen from a multitude of blondes, some of them much younger than her. She would start the following week, and she'd be well paid. She then placed them one next to the other on the couch. She turned on music and gazed at them with certitude, and spread out her hair.

"And now, a private show! Let's say that you're the jury, OK? You'll see my number from beginning to end, just as I performed it for the audition."

Fred sank into the couch, smiling amused, and Edi sat on the edge tense, his palms tight between his knees and his glasses steamy from the humidity that had suddenly engulfed his living room, the room becoming the stage for a show he never could have imagined.

Mimi let herself go in the narrow space between the tiny table and the TV, careful not to turn anything over. She alternated between moments of classical ballet and devilish modern dance; she performed pirouettes and dramatic movements, met the air or crawled along the carpet, threw her legs about with ease, shielding the two spectators, and all the while she managed to maintain her smile and force, looking them in the eye, now one, then the other, seductive and self-confident, as if they were the committee that her employment contract depended on.

The two men could hear her labored breathing and saw her muscles throb, and when she went around on her toes with her shoulders above her head, her short, pleated skirt pulsed like an accordion played by the force of the wind, giving rise to a sort of draft with strawberry aromas that hit Edi straight in the face, freezing his forehead. A long strand of Mimi's hair floated for some seconds through the air above the couch and landed on one of Edi's knees. He almost heard the thud. Mimi finished her performance and bowed before their feet. The music kept on thumping from the speakers long after Edi had run, unsure on his feet, to the bathroom.

Fred pulled Mimi onto his knees, kissed her and took her up to the bedroom, swinging her in his arms like a bird that had barely survived a long exhausting flight, and he closed the door behind him. Mimi laughed excitedly and screamed with pleasure. She quieted down later, after she had climaxed several times, and Edi had knocked against the bedroom wall with a shoe, saying that he had to go to work the next day and they'd both do well not to upset him, because in the end, ballet or no ballet, they were there because of him.

When Mimi went to shower, the light in the living room was still on. Edi had never stayed up late at night till then. They had surely gone overboard; perhaps Edi had really gotten upset this time, or something had happened. She had thought to go see what he was doing, to appease him if need be, so she wrapped a towel around her waist and knocked discretely on the door. Edi turned off his light immediately and was totally quiet, meaning that he wanted to be left alone. Mimi gave up. She went back to the bedroom, stuck herself against Fred and went happily to sleep.

Edi didn't go to work the following day. In the morning, he called his boss, telling him he had a cold and he'd rather stay home. A first since the bank had hired him. The manager had told him to take care of himself on his day off. He lay all day with the blanket over his head.

Edi refused to eat and speak; he didn't even drink the chamomile tea with lemon that Mimi bought him. But he got up at night and went to 47th Street, taking advantage of the fact that Fred and Mimi had gone to the city and he didn't need to converse with them or give them any explanations.

Fred felt embarrassed about the scene and regretted acting on his attraction to Mimi's exuberance.

"Let's be more careful not to upset Edi. A good and sensitive soul overall... He tolerates us with angelic patience."

"But we're also enriching his life," Mimi consoled Fred. "Without us, he'd die of boredom and sadness. In the end, he's very lucky to have us. I bet he didn't go to work today because he was too full of energy. And he can't take a fulfilling and cheerful life. It drags him down."

"Exactly. Let's protect him a bit. We're loud, we're too much for him. We've turned his life upside down; he was happy the way he lived before. We've talked about this already. What you take as happiness might be a torment to another."

"We'll move out soon. He'll go back to his old life then. His grand old life, what can I say!"

"And what theater are you working in?" Fred couldn't help but ask.

"What does it matter? They liked me, they took me, they'll pay me and that's that. The contract begins exactly on my last day in Soho. Maybe I'll rebuild my career. Who knows?"

There was no point in asking her what career she meant.

Back then, 42nd Street had a bad reputation. The last traces of a cultural revolution lingered around Grand Central Station and Times Square, areas full of sex shops, cabarets, porn theaters, beggars and drug addicts. After the sun set, it was outright dangerous. Drug dealers, thieves and vagabonds hustled on the streets. Years later the decadent areas changed and were taken over by tourists.

The following Sunday, the salon's owner told her employees—in fact, her former employees—that she wanted to invite them to a farewell party at an Italian restaurant, one of the luxurious traditional venues of the New York haute-bourgeoisie where one had to make a reservation at least a month ahead of time and had to be quite a name in order to have a guaranteed spot. In other words, one had to have not only money, but also fame, if not some blue blood, as in Europe.

Mimi's boss had gotten on *that* list some weeks before, when through a lucky chance encounter, as often happens in New York, she'd had two music stars and a famous actor as clients. *People* magazine had given them a mention, and Fancy Soho salon showed up in all the photos. The owner even gave the paper a short interview.

Mimi was in seventh heaven about her stage debut. The possibility of dancing again, even if at a second-rate venue in a not-so-great part of New York, had overshadowed any fear related to losing her receptionist job. What's more, she was excited by the fact that she'd go to an upscale restaurant.

"My love, the waiters look like college professors, have white shirts and white carnations pinned on their buttonholes. I'm so sorry you can't come along, but I promise you that someday we'll be able to afford to eat in these places. How many lives do we have? And I'm telling you that I won't mess up this time."

Mimi mused this way whenever she found herself in states of exaltation, which Fred had given up on trying to restrain.

He'd gotten used to her euphoria and her upstart dream of a bright future tied to her prospects in a world that seemed to fit her better and better, a dream that she had slowly begun to transfer from his fragile and unsure shoulders to hers.

"As all of them have made it, and let's be honest, they're not the brightest stars in the sky, I'll make it too. I see myself at the top every night before I fall asleep. Did I tell you about the trick where you project what you want to become? While you're still awake, you should imagine yourself as you want to be. It's an exercise that you need to take seriously and do before you fall asleep. When the brain is in alpha and you can give it orders. You know, alpha, when it's not paying attention and believes anything. I read about it. I'm commanding my brain to make me rich and famous. What do you say about this?"

Fred loved her, alpha or not, with her little, restless behind, tirelessly searching for success, day-in-and-out.

On the morning of the day of the party, Mimi put cn an avocado mask, got her hair and nails done carefully and went to Bloomingdale's in the afternoon, having made up her mind to buy the most expensive outfit. Jessica had told her that on the ground level of the store, in the cosmetics department, she could get her make-up done for free, so she sat down on the chair of a young stylist who moved like a ballerina, saying that she'd like to buy a foundation cream and lipstick that would fit her complexion, and she fell into his delicate hands.

Then she passed by the perfume counter and tried a dab of Channel No. 5, after which she went directly to the first floor, tried on seven dresses and chose the most spectacular one. She paid with a credit card she had received with difficulty two months earlier, staring with a sense of superiority at the short saleswoman dressed in an impeccable suit. The woman put her dress and hanger in a plastic bag, then carefully placed it in the well-known "big brown bag," the label of the store that Mimi had long coveted.

Look at these pigs how they live, thought Mimi as she tried on a splendid pair of shoes that matched the color of her new dress. The shoes had thin high heels made to rule the world. She also bought an evening purse, putting all the receipts away in her wallet after asking every department what their return policy was, to make sure that she'd have 30 days to return the items in case she changed her mind.

She left the store with the haughty feeling of being a wealthy woman. And kept banging the "big" and "medium brown bags" with her legs, as a symbol of wealth. A doorman held the door open for her. She almost felt like giving him a tip, calling for a taxi and forgetting about everything, but she changed her mind and went down Park Avenue, where she remembered there was a Staples store and bought a bunch of adhesive paper rolls. She then took the subway, restless to get home before Fred, who had told her that he'd be at the library until 4:00.

When she got back, Fred found her gluing adhesive paper on the soles of her new shoes.

"What are you doing?" he asked her distractedly, while putting his books on the bed next to her dress that was spread out in all its glory.

Mimi looked at him and suddenly saw him differently.

"Why do you walk hunchbacked?"

"What do you mean?"

"It's like you're smaller, I don't know. Shorter. Straighten your back, look how you're walking," she said petulantly. "You look as if you carry the world on your shoulders. God knows what worries you have."

"Maybe I do."

"What can I say? I carry worries and responsibilities but still keep my posture."

"I'm walking normally, as I always have," Fred answered calmly. "What are you doing with those shoes? Are you adjusting your grandiose stature?"

"Don't be mean now. I need to return these shoes. They cost $300. I'm wearing them tonight and that's it. They won't take them back if they see that they've been worn."

"And are you sure they'll take them back if you stick paper to their soles?"

"Yes, Fred, I'm sure. That's how it is in this country," said Mimi, and she pushed him out of the bedroom. "I'll put on a show for you in a bit. Go away."

She put on a pair of cheap stockings, which weren't visible anyway since the dress touched the ground. She put on the shoes and slipped away the receipt for the dress that lengthened her waist and emphasized her round breasts (which Fred had said would never age). She looked into the tiny mirror hanging in the closet—the effect was grand, despite her not seeing her own feet.

She appeared several minutes later by the living room door, beaming. She walked as a model on the runway, flinging her feet up excitedly, stepping heavily as to make a mark. Only that the living room was small. After a couple of steps Mimi stopped before Fred, placed a hand on her thigh and balanced her rhinestone-laden purse, waiting for his reaction.

"Won't it be tough for you to walk in those shoes? They seem so high," said Fred.

"It only seems so," she answered. "Is that all you can say?"

"Oh, you look great! But I don't think you need to put that necklace on. The dress is heavy enough," he added tactfully.

"I like it."

"Very well, then leave it."

Mimi huffed, unsatisfied.

"What's wrong with this necklace? Is it too kitsch? Or does it go contrary to your idea of simplicity?"

"I didn't mean to upset you."

Fred extended his hand to her with the desire to pull her onto the couch, but Mimi took a step back.

"For your information, I've become stylish. You don't need to teach me or tutor me anymore. I can figure things out on my own from now on."

"It was simply an opinion. Don't make a mountain out of a molehill. You're very beautiful. I don't even know why I'm letting you go by yourself."

"And I don't know what I'm doing here," Mimi shot back.

She turned around on her heels and headed to the bedroom, stepping less heavily than before.

Fred followed her. He closed the door, embraced her when she least expected it, and opened the zipper of her dress, which went down to her ass. He bit her lightly under her neck, feeling his erection grow as he squeezed her breasts. He dragged her to the edge of the bed and slipped his legs between the opening of her dress, which had fallen to the ground.

"Control yourself, Fred. I need to leave. You're wrinkling my clothes. And don't touch my hair. It took me two hours to get it done."

Mimi fought back, more indecisive with every word.

"Bend down," he murmured in her ear. "I won't ruin anything."

"And be careful not to tear the receipt. I need to take the dress back. It's very expensive."

He penetrated her from behind as he felt the sharp ends of her shoes caress his thighs, and he finished violently, sinking his knees in the soft mattress, his hands clenching her buttocks, two apples unusually big and white.

The restaurant was indeed elegant and very expensive, but the waiters didn't have carnations in their button-holes. The salon owner booked a round table for eight by the window, where one could see the lighted tops of skyscrapers and stores' incandescent billboards with advertisements. Mimi got there last and was unanimously admired. Jessica saved her a seat next to her.

As it happened, only women worked at the Soho salon. At the other tables there were only women too, and everyone seemed as if they were having a good time in the absence of men. One wouldn't come across a scene like this in most Romanian restaurants, thought Mimi as she looked around. Women were either more eman-cipated in America, or more numerous, or more single. There was a relaxed atmosphere; candles flickered near bowls with floating white orchids; discussions were in low voices, the waiters moved about silently, and the music could hardly be heard from speakers inside the walls that were lined with honey-colored silk.

It was a world of undertones, beautiful and content. Here and there, the silverware clinking against porcelain dishes, the crystal glasses barely touching in a toast, or the laughter of a woman melodiously rang out. The mission of the place seemed to be the maintaining of balances, an ode to equilibrium, and, indeed, any sort of dissonance, stridency or excess, were all impossible there.

Too bad Fred couldn't see how one had to live, what was worth striving for. She was ready to declare on the spot that this state of satisfaction would from that point on be obligatory for humanity. Or at least for the two of them. She didn't know whether these were communist or bourgeois ideals. But wherever they came from, they were healthy; they were good for the body and soul.

She had finished her endive salad with Roquefort cheese, and left only the vegetables that had been served next to a generous filet mignon on the side. She'd prudently ordered it *medium rare* to make the best impression, though she'd never liked red meat. Afterward, she excused herself and went to the bathroom. She wanted to adjust the label which she'd slipped under the dress. It had loosened, and poked at her sharply.

The restroom was the same story: green marble, couches, mirrors, white orchids, music flowing from the walls, perfume in the air. An old hag who'd had plenty of plastic surgeries and a thick gold necklace on which hung a dragon with emerald eyes came out of a stall as large as their kitchen. Mimi wanted to smile at her, but the woman didn't care to respond, or perhaps she couldn't open her stretched-out jaws.

As Mimi was going back to her table, she saw some public telephones in the hallway and hurried to call Fred to give him a first impression about the place where every extravagance seemed normal. Water from a fountain trickled through polished stones and tiny plants, giving the impression of a miniature Japanese garden. Her dress rustled in agreement with the general hum of the place.

She didn't see the wide hole in the dark marble on the floor. She stepped into nothingness. Her right leg twisted and broke on the spot in two places, and Mimi collapsed, screaming in pain and terrifying the entire restaurant. On hearing her cry, a cry that had never been heard there, cooks ran through doors, their white hats flying; waiters, bartenders and head waiters desperately ran to her, not knowing what was going on. Mimi was straining on the floor, her body contorted; one of her legs had been caught in a drain.

"Ambulance! Call the ambulance," cried the general manager, his eyes bulging. "Where are those idiots?"

The idiots were two plumbers who had been called to check the drains and forgotten to put the lid back on the one that Mimi had slipped in.

Jessica went with her to the hospital and called Fred to explain what happened.

A few days after the operation, Jessica gave her the business card of a lawyer and instructed Mimi what to do.

"Call him. I told him everything. He's accepted your case. He's a ferocious guy, you'll see. He'll skin them alive."

"I can't believe that I fall into a hole like an idiot and they pay," Mimi laughed, her leg in traction. "Whenever I fell, my mother would spank me to be more careful the next time, and you're telling me that here they'll reward me? They were already being too nice paying for my dinner."

"What world are you living in?" asked Jessica annoyed. "What payment? Two-three thousand bucks? And what did you get from it all? The owner of the salon probably didn't pay anything, but you have a broken leg. Didn't you hear about that old lady that burned herself from coffee at McDonald's and ended up with millions of dollars? That's how it goes. And this is an expensive and prosperous worldwide restaurant chain. Sue them and ask for hundreds of thousands of dollars. But the lawyer knows best."

The lawyer, Mr. John Sheppard—a man of about 50—came in the day after Mimi had called him following Jessica's advice, though she was convinced he'd laugh at her. He was dressed in an elegant suit with a vest and a handkerchief matching his tie in his chest pocket; he was perfectly "presentable," according to

Mimi's criterion. He placed his chair next to her bed, put his suitcase down and extended his hand jovially, asking her in passing how she felt before getting to the point again. Time is money. And it was obvious that he didn't have time.

He presented things as simply and clearly as possible. In his vision, these were tragic times for Mimi, an emigrant who'd struggled to survive, ran from Ceaușescu's dictatorship to start from scratch in a better world that she knew placed the needs of the individual and the individual's wellbeing first and foremost. Since she'd arrived in New York, she'd worked hard, so as to finally fulfill her dream of continuing her career as a ballerina—her destiny—which had brought her prestige not only in her birth country, but in Paris as well. She had just signed a contract with a theater on Broadway when, suddenly, due to the negligence and irresponsibility of an upscale restaurant, which one would suppose would protect rather than maim its clients, her dream fell apart, her future gravely compromised and the quality of her life altered. A promising ballerina becomes handicapped only because she wanted to spend her hard-earned money at a festive dinner that celebrated her artistic debut (among other things—that was Mr. Sheppard's spin) in a country where everyone's dreams come true and aren't checked by the incompetence of money-hungry restaurateurs who neglect the protection and security of their clients in their haste to fill up their pockets.

Despite Mimi's protests, ever poorer in comparison to Mr. Sheppard's eloquence and pathos, the story became increasingly credible and dramatic, culminating in the final number that fell like a ton of rocks: one million dollars.

"One million? Are you crazy?" said Mimi incredulously.

"Pardon me?" Sheppard pretended not to hear.

He continued his case: this hard-working and devoted woman was also the only provider. Mind the word: provider!—a strong and powerful word in this culture—supporting her husband, a great dissident writer whose books would have enriched world culture had he had the leisure to write them. Look how a family winds up suddenly broke, without any source of income or chance for a future. Whoever is to blame should pay, ensure these honest people a decent existence worthy of their experience and dreams, which they've been irresponsibly deprived of.

Mimi melted. She wanted to weep, and to hold back her tears, she stared at Sheppard's shiny handkerchief with its blue stripes. She had learned, as a child, to keep her sneeze in by squeezing her nose and concentrating her glance on an object: so she tried the same trick to hold back her tears. She signed the papers that were given to her; the lawyer assured her that he wouldn't ask for any fee: he'd only take 35% of the sum that she'd win from the trial, more proof that he was going in to win. Sheppard also told her to ask for copies of the surgery report, all the X-rays and any other medical documents from the hospital. Then he got out a small camera and took pictures from different angles of Mimi's swollen leg hanging in traction.

Mimi wanted to fix her hair, or perhaps apply some lipstick, but the lawyer stopped her with one abrupt wave of his hand. There was no point in making herself look good. Mimi burst into tears. He then took a photo of her tears trickling down her face and in a low voice, wished that she gets well soon. Loudly, very loudly, he told her he would be in touch about the first court appearance.

Sometimes people speak loudly and clearly when talking to immigrants, thinking they have trouble understanding.

Mimi kept on sniveling. She was confused and suddenly felt an intense longing for Fred. He was the only calm and stable reference point in her hysterical quicksand world.

They let her go home a couple of days afterward, but she'd have to use crutches for three months. When she returned to the apartment, a huge basketful of flowers awaited her. Fred hastened to tell her that her lawyer had sent them along with a tiny note stating that in two weeks the trial would begin.

The contract with the Broadway theater was terminated, and they practically lived on welfare. One night, Fred gave Edi his mother's ring, which he'd saved for desperate situations, and told him to sell it on 47th Street to cover their expenses.

Jessica visited her sometimes; all three sat on the living room couch drinking wine, and Fred would pick up cat hair from her sweaters. This gesture wouldn't be noticed by either of the two women. Fred played Bach and Mozart for them, and they'd ask him to tell them about novels or events from the lives of famous artists.

Jessica seemed to have lost some weight, and the acne on her face had disappeared. She'd gotten rid of the brown hazelnut mole on her chin, but continued to pull on her hair, chew gum and drink tons of water. She seemed more put together since she'd started working again as a social worker in a Manhattan hospital, though she complained that she missed the salon, a job that fit her better.

She'd agreed to appear as a witness in the restaurant trial, convinced that Mimi would obtain a handsome compensation, but she didn't know the huge sum the lawyer promised to get for Mimi, which Mimi dreaded and which amused Fred to no end. They never spoke about this. They jumped into the lawyer's game without hoping for anything, Mimi so as not to disappoint the lawyer and Jessica, and Fred only insofar as to support Mimi's morale. She limped miserably through the house, incapable, once in her life, of planning her next move.

Paradoxically, Fred was doing well. He was writing several hours a day while Mimi watched TV, read magazines or slept. He went grocery shopping, vacuumed, helped her wash dishes; he had suddenly become very busy and full of responsibilities, but still was inspired and in good spirits, strong and in control.

He had found a comfortable position so they could make love without touching her stalactite leg, which they moved carefully on one part or another, while they made love. So Mimi declared herself satisfied, all in all.

The trial lasted several months. Mr. Sheppard sent a limousine to take her to and from the court each time. Mimi showed up in her crutches with the face of an angel fallen right from paradise, thumped on the lane between the seats in the courtroom with her crutches, and stared everyone in the eye while they glanced down with shame, pity or simply because they'd been educated that it's not polite to stare at a beautiful woman.

Mr. Sheppard was indeed a beast that could horrify or crush you, talents he would put to good use in convincing the jury of the pressing necessity to recompense commensurate to the crime. The prosecutors were also aggressive and had made up their minds not to offer a single penny to the injured victim—Mimi—whom they accused of carelessness. Perhaps she drank too much? Or perhaps she'd slipped and fallen into the drain? The shoes were to blame, they concluded: slippery soles. She would have fallen anyway, she would have broken her leg anyway, with or without the uncovered drain, they claimed.

At this crucial moment, Mimi brought out the pair of shoes with adhesive paper glued to their soles and gave them to the jurors, who passed them over from one to another, nodding knowingly. With those soles, one couldn't even slip on the Rockefeller Center ice rink. Then she told them, humbly and with eyes wet with shame, how she had glued those strips to the shoes the day before the party hoping to return them to the Bloomingdale's the following day, unable to afford something so expensive. Her accent was as convincing as the adhesive band on the soles. While they listened to her confession, the jurors' eyes also watered, and Mr. Sheppard stared at her stupefied. Jackpot!

"I won the trial by myself," Mimi would say later, unhappy with the percentage that the lawyer had received according to their agreement.

Only when she'd first made the deal, Mimi would've accepted anything. She hadn't believed an iota of Sheppard's delirium, capped off with that resounding *$1,000,000.*

She wouldn't win one million dollars. The lawyers consulted one another and agreed that $600,000 would be reasonable to put an end to the conflict. They settled with the condition that Mimi wouldn't make the verdict public and wouldn't mention the accident and the name of the restaurant to the media, would never refer to the place under any circumstances, nor to the way in which the unfortunate event had transpired. Unfortunate, but which had transformed her overnight into a rich woman.

The money went into her bank account mere days after she threw out her crutches. She finished her recuperation and physical therapy program, and her legs regained their vigor and form. Perfect for the race that was about to unfold.

Mr. Sheppard, who had also cashed a fat check, sent her a basketful of flowers and a postcard, in which he congratulated her on her better health and invited her to lunch at Da Silvano.

"For a while, I wanted to give up high heels," Mimi told him as the waiter brought them warm bread with olives flavored in all sorts of condiments. "As for the ballet slippers, I couldn't care less for them. You know what I mean! I'm not so naïve. I think you realize this."

Sheppard tried to smile, but could only grimace and raise an eyebrow, hinting to her that jokes and commentaries of this kind were inappropriate, even between them. Mimi understood and acted with professional restraint.

The lunch progressed monotonously. She ordered a tuna salad and *fettucine alfredo*, drank only plain water and spoke in a controlled manner, with an elegant but cold tone. Sheppard ordered a glass of Chianti, and after, the waiter brought them espresso and biscotti. Before asking for the check, he looked at her closely once again and said bluntly:

"It's a large sum. You know you'll have to pay taxes, too. Have you thought about what you'll do with the money?"

Not prepared with an answer and thinking that he wanted to test her, Mimi replied vaguely:

"What everyone does."

"And what does everyone do?" Sheppard appeared sincerely curious.

"I'll get a house and a car."

It seemed to her that Sheppard smiled ironically. She added:

"Then I'll see if there's anything left and try something else."

Sheppard relaxed, ordered another glass of wine, pushed the check to the edge of the table as a hint that he wasn't looking to leave anytime soon, gazed at her with concern and whispered as charmingly as possible:

"I think you need an adviser."

"I have Fred. We'll discuss it with each other."

"You didn't understand me." Sheppard went on without blinking. "Our husband is an artist, like you," he hastened to say. "I meant a financial expert. Money needs to be administered with care, invested intelligently so as to produce the largest return possible," he explained calmly.

"To tell you frankly, my dream is to open a beauty salon. I think I'd be very good at that. I know how it works. I'm a professional. I have experience and most of all, I have ideas," she confessed, crossing her legs, propping her elbows on the table and glancing at him obliquely with an old sense of complicity, feeling herself in control again. "Instinct tells me that I could hit the jackpot now."

"That's something else altogether! We're talking about a business," said Sheppard. He looked at her admiringly. "Should I look for a location?"

"But I want the best location!"

"And you need a solid partner. Let me think. I might be able to come up with a proposal soon."

They each ordered a digestive, a Limoncello, perfect for this occasion, sweet and smooth, to celebrate the plan and shook hands. At the end of their meeting, Sheppard kissed her on the cheek.

Crazy months followed. Sheppard kept his promise and helped her launch her business sooner than she had expected. He found her a rich old man willing to go into business with her, an owner of multiple companies going through a third marriage with a young Russian who had stimulated his interest in Eastern Europe, where he hoped to extend his businesses and expand his fortunes. He put her in contact with realtors, accountants and financial experts that Mimi soon learned to communicate with; she hinted to them that she wanted to play hard and that they'd receive a good reward if they could get a prosperous business running.

The phones rang constantly at Edi's. Everyone was looking for Mimi.

"You've become very popular," Fred said to her with neither irony nor reproach. "Who are all these people?"

"My love, you have to understand. America is the perfect place of intermediaries. You can't take a step without them. Lawyers, brokers, agents... In our country, we used to fight institutions by ourselves and lose. Here, they fight for you. It's true that it costs, but at least they win, you saw! Just as you need a literary agent to get to a publisher for a mere book, well, you can only imagine how many middlemen I need!"

"I can imagine," Fred murmured ironically, her words "mere book" having hit him under the belt.

"How words slip away," Mimi cried suddenly. "I said 'our country' thinking about Romania. We need to be more careful about what we say, darling. Our country is America now!"

She raised her chin and pushed her chest forward as if she had just heard the national anthem somewhere in the background. "Period!"

They made love more rarely. Mimi was either too tired or too excited. Sometimes, during the act, she'd wind up thinking about some offer that had come her way that day, or she'd calculate in her mind how much this or that would cost. Other times she wouldn't finish. She'd try to hide that from Fred, who'd pretend that he didn't notice.

She had become important, had meetings and viewings of all sorts of places and apartments. She was gone all day long, and when she returned at night, she rushed to Fred to tell him how things were evolving. She spoke loud and quickly, stepped firmly, made grand gestures, laughed with zest, was on a diet without sugar and cholesterol, despite being perfectly healthy, had begun to drink several bottles of water a day, bought herself elegant outfits and arranged her hair according to photographs in business women's magazines that displayed women with white teeth, sharp expressions, gratified faces, long throats and strong, self-confident airs.

Fred moved into the background again. She no longer asked him how his writing was going or if he was progressing with the book, and he went about his business, happy that he was kept apart from the agitation that had come upon her. But he felt somewhat intimidated by the changes.

By the end of the year, their lives would change radically. Mimi became the owner of a beauty salon on Fifth Avenue that extended to two floors and which she had bought in partnership with the old entrepreneur recommended by Sheppard. On one side, she invested; on the other, she borrowed from the bank, as she was counseled to do. She already had 20 employees. A broker administered the finances, an accountant transacted, a lawyer supervised her contracts and opportunities continued to arise. Jessica was her office manager. Jessica had lost weight and was seeing a computer programmer with cat allergies, so she'd given her tomcat away. The acne on her face had completely disappeared, and she no longer pulled on her hair.

They moved from Edi's into a spacious apartment on Central Park West. Mimi bought a black Mercedes, her dream car, although Fred had told her that he had no desire to drive it.

They changed their wardrobe once they became members and donors of all sorts of exclusive clubs, including the Metropolitan Museum of Art, MOMA and the Guggenheim; all these museums had added their names to their lists of patrons. They ate at upscale restaurants at night and afterward went to the theater or to see a film. They participated in all sorts of charity events, which bored Fred but which Mimi took in intensely.

"Wouldn't you like to learn to play golf, my love?"

"Golf?" exclaimed Fred, and he laughed heartily.

"Yes, golf! Why does it seem so silly to you?" snapped Mimi. "All well-bred men play it. The best connections in the upper classes happen on golf courses. In essence, you'd be going in the same direction as me for a change. And I don't think it's that difficult either, you know. Fresh air. It would do you good to get out a bit."

Fred continued to laugh.

The mix of candor and ambition in her was seductive, but a thorn had pricked his heart and would settle and grow there as, day by day, Mimi would push the envelope more and more and miraculously get more rabbits, pigeons, aces of clubs and stock shares out of the hat.

"How can you not believe in miracles when they've happened to you?" said Mimi, rearranging the antiques in their large apartment, where Fred didn't feel at home. "I think you're too skeptical. That's it. These doubts only stop you. I know you'll tell me that only fools don't doubt themselves. But I don't think that inertia is the privilege of those who are smart."

"Hasty changes that come too fast make some folks seem inert," murmured Fred from his writing desk.

"Transformations take time, need time to settle and be understood... accepted. One can't jump into a diver's suit before knowing how deep the water is."

"Whew!" Mimi grew indignant. "We're so different. But this is why we're attracted to each other, isn't that so, my love?" She tempted him with her piercing stare, practicing her tolerance. "I mean to say that even differences are exciting. Up to a point!"

Then she slammed something down with an ostentatious look, to get across that her patience was starting to wear off.

Little by little, Fred stopped joining her at fashionable parties under the pretext that he had to write, and she didn't protest, sometimes finding him either too grumpy or too ironic or indifferent. His demeanor didn't exactly agree with the business environment where everyone smiles continuously, speaks formally while exchanging business cards, and lives on the surface—though it was exactly from this superficiality that the most solid business associations came from.

A year later, Mimi would also buy a luxurious apartment in Palm Beach, Florida, where she brought her parents from Romania to stay. Fulfilled dreams didn't tire her; the lightning-speed of her ascent didn't make her dizzy or afraid. Her feet were firmly planted on the ground and her mind was clear.

The *Mimosa* Beauty Salon blossomed by the day. Her clients were wealthy women, willing to try anything in exchange for the promises of camouflaging old age. Guided by Sheppard, Mimi had gone into other businesses as well. He also tried to play a different role in her life.

One weekend, John Sheppard—John, as he'd asked her from the beginning to call him—invited her to go with him to Nantucket, an exclusive island for rich folks who had vacation homes there. It seemed like it would be a good chance to get to know her mysterious partner, Adam Morgan, better. Old and very rich, he lived far from the spotlight, avoided socialization and had retreated to his Nantucket estate, where for several years, he hadn't been able to play golf or go yachting. Mimi had only seen him once and didn't even remember what he looked like. John was the intermediary between them.

Morgan had invested in *Mimosa*, and it seemed that he and John had other businesses as well, about which only John and her financial counselors knew in detail. She put herself completely in their hands, trusted them. She was totally absorbed in her elite spa in Manhattan and didn't pay much attention to the financial aspect.

"What you put money in, how you move it around, what you invest in—these details don't interest me. I'm not good at that and I don't have time. I only want to know what I've made in the end," Mimi always claimed.

And the profit grew like an inflated ball. Fred had tried several times to tell her that it wasn't a good idea to go into too many businesses she didn't know much about, or let other people completely control them, but Mimi calmed him using a maternal tone:

"My love, you write! Numbers aren't for you. You deserve to enjoy their results only. Don't worry, John and his people are experts, and God knows very well, they take their share. The world moves are dictated by financial interests. Mother said that love passes through the stomach. Well, we have to update that. It passes through the stock exchange: a good share run improves the appetite. And the better you eat, the hungrier you get."

Fred looked at her as if she were an alien. He almost couldn't believe that the woman with the cold reasoning of a predator slept languorously by him in bed, submitting herself meekly to his sexual moods. Or perhaps this too was part of the calculation. The thought always paralyzed him.

After a four-hour drive from New York, John and Mimi took a ferry from Hyannis, Massachusetts to Nantucket.

"A preservation for rare animals," she'd tell Fred upon returning. "Everyone was tall, beautiful, had blonde children with blue eyes and white socks, everyone was pristine but modest, my love, modest. The women don't wear any jewelry. They respect nature, eat organically, drive their help home at night. The wealthier, the more modest. Clothed simply, in pastel colors. All the houses were the same nuances of gray. No fast food, no malls, nothing—only small boutiques, cobblestone streets, yards overflowing with flowers, small family restaurants, clubs where it costs a fortune to be a member. Old money. Style. Class. Everything's minimalistic—you would have liked it—no nonsense. You pay quite a lot of money to live in a small home without air conditioning, TV or a dishwasher. It's like a statement, you see? They don't want to flaunt their wealth. Perfidy, you'll say. Pharisees. In any case though, they have big houses by the shore, all gray. We need to go there together. We can afford it."

"Melville is enough for me."

"Who's that?"

"The chronicler of whales. To me, Nantucket is tied to *Moby Dick*."

"Ah, I think I saw the movie when I was young. That's where it was filmed?"

"Read the book if you want to learn more about Nantucket."

"I didn't see whales. But there were millionaire sharks everywhere. You know what I mean."

"And where did you sleep overnight?" Fred asked her out-of-the-blue.

"At the *White Elephant*. A hotel that also has a spa. I'll tell you more some other time," Mimi evaded. "I need to run now. An army of termites waits for me at the office: after they tell me what my gains are, they'll hurry to devour the larger part of it. I don't complain. I like the jungle. Look: I've begun talking like you!"

"And that's bad?"

"These folks aren't made for metaphors. You need to speak to them as clearly as possible, in simple statements."

"You amaze me. You've begun to despise them?"

"No. I've begun to understand them. And I want to make myself perfectly understood."

The meeting with Morgan had left her in a fog. The old man had not bothered to welcome them. His wife had died, he lived alone, and several servants took care of him, his huge house and his luxurious garden, which descended to the ocean. On the front lawn, there was a large statue of a Buddha surrounded by yellow and orange flowers that sprung from Thai-style clay vases. A personal assistant dressed in white, or perhaps she was a nurse, led them to the glass terrace where Morgan was reading on a rocking chair in front of the window. He barely raised his eyes when they came in. An equally old black dog slept by his feet. The dog didn't blink either.

"I'm scared of dogs," Mimi whispered into John's ear, nearly touching him with her lips.

"Not of them you should be afraid," he replied calmly.

The rooms they passed through were decorated with paintings in heavy frames. Egyptian, Asian and African art was displayed on shelves, consoles, tables, even on the floor. The house seemed ready for a show or a move: as if a private museum had just bought the space and brought all its valuable objects there.

Morgan invited them to sit down. The assistant asked them what they'd like to have, the dog lay comfortably on the Iranian carpet, and Mimi nearly stepped on a Roman crest placed right by her armchair.

"So… How's everything going?" asked Morgan, but he didn't expect any answer. He stared at Mimi and his lips mimed what, in the old days, would have been seduction: "I couldn't pick a more beautiful partner."

Mimi whispered and wanted to say something, but Morgan stopped her with a glance. The assistant came with a large tray of cool drinks, coffee and biscotti. Morgan motioned at her, and the woman returned with an envelope and a fountain pen, which she handed to Sheppard as if they were sacred sacrifices.

"The contract renewals," John said to Mimi. "Formalities. You only need to sign. Everything's been checked by lawyers. All is well."

Morgan followed her with an indifferent smile as she speed-read the pages, hitting the Mont Blanc pen rhythmically on the Louis XV desk in a dense silence where only the heavy breathing of the dog and the ocean's waves swishing in the distance could be heard. At some point, it seemed to Sheppard and Morgan that she hesitated. The dog growled and Mimi raised her eyes, smiled to the two men as if she'd suddenly just had a revelation, and signed her name emphatically where she had been told to.

"Good luck! Ever forward!" said Mimi, sure of herself, but no one answered.

The assistant reappeared immediately, took the papers and disappeared with them.

Morgan invited them to dinner, but warned that he wouldn't participate; he was tired and not hungry.

They refused, thanked him and left in silence, just as they had come.

They lodged at *The White Elephant*. John clarified things to her on the way to the hotel. Morgan was one of New York's sacred monsters. Cultured, he spoke several languages, played the piano, wrote poetry, was a concert-goer and art collector, had traveled throughout the world and now had been forced by old age to retreat to Nantucket, where he continued to guard his wealth and even grow it. He had no heirs. At this news, Mimi jumped and her look grew slightly subtler as she imagined herself adopted by Morgan for a moment and, as such, set atop the pyramid.

Sheppard went on: he had made money in real estate while very young, had taken over his family's successful company and continued to invest, make speculations and get involved in the Brazilian coffee business. In the 1960s he traveled through Europe where he bought works by Goya, El Greco, Matisse and Magritte, which he sold at auctions. Some claimed that his moves in the art world weren't exactly kosher. What's certain is that he accumulated inestimable wealth. What Mimi saw in his home were merely remnants that he couldn't bear to part with. Blake, Delacroix, Tintoretto…

Morgan had been a handsome man. Even now he was hypnotic. He stood up straight, still had thick hair, blue eyes, elegant hands with long fingers. A womanizer? He had been once, but how could one not be in his place? His eyes still sparkled, but desire seemed to have been replaced by cynicism; curiosity had fallen into disillusionment. He had even written in one of his poems:

Old age has disappointed me.
No treachery is more than this
Except the Father's to the Son,
When he sent him out to the seas
To gather all the broken boats
And bring them to the shore.

"Beautiful words," Mimi concluded. "Spoiled by fate. Too bad I didn't know him better. And earlier!" she sniggered lightly and quickly went on: "I think Fred would like him. He is, in a way, his type…" She fanned out her hair in the wind, whispering: "But he's strong and doesn't seem to leave anything unfinished."

"Who? Fred?" asked John maliciously while arranging her scarf, which the wind had blown over her bare shoulders. "Back to business now. We didn't come here to admire the masters of European painting or just to sign papers. The *White Elephant* has everything it needs: an exclusive spa and fitness club, plastic surgery and rejuvenation rooms, perfect for your future investment. Morgan has arranged for you to rent a part of the hotel for the *Mimosa II* clinic. Between us, he's the owner of the complex. Think about how many of your clients in Manhattan have homes on the island.

They stay here over the summer. Treatments are paid for in cash. Prices are double what they are in New York. You can even sell your argil creams, your mud packages, everything that comes to mind."

"Isn't it too early for me to expand? Too risky?"

"Riskier is *not* to do this deal," Sheppard said wryly. "I've been working on it for several months."

"And why am I finding out only now?"

"You're finding out at the right time," he replied, softening his voice. "I didn't want you to worry your adorable head about accounting details, negotiations, marketplace prospects. But I admit to having planned for it to happen this way. It's been ten years since we won the trial. Today."

"You're right," Mimi grew luminous. "A blessed day!"

After the meeting in the business hall of the hotel with all the staff involved in the transaction, Mimi oscillated between pleasant fatigue and excitement after once again signing all the papers that came her way.

Sheppard's eyes devoured her.

"You're fantastic," he said, hardly restraining himself from embracing her. "Seldom have I seen a more courageous and inventive woman moving so dizzyingly fast with such force and grace. Someday you'll have to write a book, a success guide for businesswomen. You know all the tricks."

"Ha! I don't write books, John. Speak to Fred. He could make me the main character in one of his. Or maybe I'm not good enough for him? I'm joking."

In the evening, they celebrated at the hotel's restaurant. Sheppard had ordered a sumptuous meal in an art deco private room with a Braque painting on the front wall, small cactus flowers in an ice cube filled halfway with shells.

"I do afford to start off with oysters, caviar and lobster."

"Ah, John, you overwhelm me as usual."

"You're the overwhelming one," he replied, taking her hand and kissing it while he stared into her eyes. "Ravishing!"

"America has fulfilled my dreams. Let's drink to this country, then—for our fabulous New York and for you, John, through whom God has extended to me the most generous hand," Mimi toasted with bravado, aware that if Fred had heard her, he would have chastised her immediately for the cheap pathos.

So what? Mimi was Mimi; she wasn't afraid, as before, that she might mess up. A rich and pretty famous woman to boot, she could allow herself to be as she wished, when she wished.

They drank a good deal, ate quite well, praised each other and made new plans for the future. As they were about to part, Sheppard caught her by the waist and held her tight against him in the hallway where their suites neighbored each other. Mimi was surprised for a moment, hesitating between letting herself soften against him and politely denying him. She pushed him lightly just when he was about to kiss her.

"John, you're a great guy. I won't lie to you. I've been attracted to you since the day you came to my hospital room and offered me your handkerchief with blue stripes to wipe my tears—in which I blew my nose, anyhow—I remember your face then! I was so embarrassed. I lay with my leg hanging from the ceiling, when I most wanted to dance for you. I remember it all!"

Sheppard had gotten very excited; all he wanted was to pull her into his room. It was the normal dénouement to an abnormally successful day that could bring them great financial gains. But Mimi continued her monologue with her seductive smile, her well-acted naiveté. She twisted her body as the words kept their rhythm with the swinging of her small rhinestone bag and her delicate shoes with sharp tips. She dallied around, exciting him even more.

"I would have liked us to be more than friends, John. We would have been more than perfect. An invincible couple. But you have a wife."

"What does it matter? We don't want to get married and have kids, do we?!"

Sheppard closed in to embrace her impatiently, but Mimi gently pushed him away.

"I can't imagine making love to a man… outside that."

"Don't be silly," smiled John, attempting again to get close to her.

"I'm not joking. If you want to get a divorce and marry me, well, that's different!"

Sheppard stared at her, stunned. Mimi kept the tension going for some moments and then burst out with laughter.

"Did you get scared?" she asked as she opened the door. "I was joking! John, business is more important than a night of lovemaking. I don't want to compromise our relationship in any way. You understand. A business relationship is enough for us. And at least we're making money from it. We have a future."

She kissed him hurriedly on the cheek, and before closing her door said to him as warmly as possible:

"And we don't know what the future will bring. We need to be aware!"

Sheppard saluted her, waving friendly and went back to his suite with his pride intact and a jolly feeling, as if he'd just lost a hundred dollars to win a million.

She entered her room and kept on smiling as she took her dress off slowly and gracefully, like a true ballerina. She was satisfied with how she'd played her scene, how she'd chosen her words. Fred would have been proud of her.

"John has a hound's sense," Mimi would say to Fred upon returning.

"Perhaps you needed just such a man," Fred wanted to answer her, but his mind wandered elsewhere. He lit his pipe, his glasses steamed, and a mad longing for his mother ravaged his chest.

3.

ANOTHER EVENING THAT FRED WOULD spend home alone. It got dark early, thanks in part to the neighboring apartment complex, which blocked their light and view toward the boulevard like a brick curtain. From their windows, Manhattan might have appeared grandiose with its silhouettes thrown against the sky or wrapped ingeniously around glass and metal giants, with storied terraces on the tops of buildings and rivers of cars beneath, fizzling out at rounds of flowers and trees on Park Avenue, differing by the season.

Fred drew the curtains slowly. Mimi had left a voice message that she'd be going to a cocktail party organized by a cosmetics company at "W."

"A recently opened luxurious hotel," she added.

She told him not to wait for her, to take his medicine and sleeping pills and go to sleep in peace.

Fred lay on the couch where, according to Mimi's warning, he'd one day grow roots. He wanted to call Jim, but remembered that Jim had not yet returned from the Art Fair in Miami.

He turned on his lamp, filled his pipe, oscillated between Styron and Celan, decided to read Styron and opened his book on his knees. Reading about other people's depressions helped him. But the letters crowded into black dots. He couldn't make out a single word. The emptiness in his chest grew larger, pressed against his diaphragm and squeezed his organs, which felt as if they were struggling to get out.

He straightened his shoulders, closed the book and pressed his hands against his chest to slow down his heartbeat. He had gotten used to the sensation of the flickering wings of a pigeon. An awareness of imponderability drowned his body. He felt his carotid artery throbbing. His cheeks burned. He sweated, though a cold wave had descended from his head to the tips of his fingers. He saw his shadow projected disproportionately by the lamplight on the wall that had been painted red according to Mimi's taste. A deformed dwarf moved along with him and held a pipe in his right hand. The phone rang and the dwarf grew scared, dropped the pipe, tripped by a seat and hastened to answer. Fred listened.

"Good news. You've just been selected by our time-share program to spend a three-day cruise in the Caribbean…"

"Hang up," whispered Fred. "Turn it off; they drive us crazy with their offers. None of it is true, they want to fool us… hang up!"

He turned on the light, put on a jacket and ran outside. The cars' headlights made the cement sparkle, as did the shiny stockings on elegant women who were headed to shows and restaurants, hanging on the arms of some ghosts with bowties. It was the time when taxis took over the city. Fred wanted to flag one down, but he realized that he'd forgotten his wallet at home. He walked toward Lexington Avenue. Some youngsters were smoking and laughing heartily in front of an Irish pub. Music blasted inside, and there was laughter and the clanking of beer mugs. The noise put him in a state of panic. It seemed to him that at any moment something extremely dangerous might happen, or that some disaster would occur.

He moved more quickly and crossed the street, bumping into plastic garbage bags that flanked the curbs. He stared into the window of a store and felt his heart sink. The dwarf was following him. He began to run, glancing now and again at the shops' windows. The dwarf ran at the same pace. Fred suddenly made a heroic decision. He stopped and turned around, determined to confront him. No trace of the dwarf. Only an old tramp wrapped in a greasy cape, with fleece gloves cut at the fingertips and two hats on his head, one on top of the other.

They stared at each other frightened. A woman in an elegant fur coat passed by, glanced down at them, raised her collar and quickened her steps. The beggar opened his toothless mouth and stretched out his hand, blessing Fred with a hoarse voice. Fred gave him a piece of crumpled paper that he found in his pocket as if he were giving him money and went away, staring back once in a while. The beggar mumbled a few words that were not too kind.

The dwarf had disappeared. He had probably gone into the subway station to surprise him, Fred thought. Now he realized that the dwarf looked like the short man who had photographed him at Rockefeller Plaza. Maybe it *was* him? But he couldn't be sure of anything. He took a turn on Madison, trod swiftly for several dozen feet on the empty boulevard, felt that he was suffocating and stopped and propped himself against a wall to calm his breathing. The dove wings had frozen under his shirt.

His friend Sam lived nearby. But Fred had forgotten his phone number; he had no way of letting him know, so he'd simply burst into his apartment, hoping that Fanny, his wife, wouldn't be home. In her presence, they needed to speak a different way. Only about nonsense. At least Mimi could take the tough subjects for a while. She'd been a good listener. Willing to learn.

He found Sam in the middle of the living room sitting on a tiny red plastic chair placed on a towel and staring straight ahead, his kippah on his head. He didn't turn his head when Fred rushed into the room greeting him loudly, creating the impression that he was much more joyful than he really was.

Fred always had to make an effort to blend in with the usually agitated mood of his friend. He could talk about anything with Sam, and not need too many words either. Sam listened more than he spoke, but he always left Fred feeling calmer than when he'd come in, with the feeling that there was nothing to be done and all blame lay elsewhere.

Sam knew how to counter Fred's lamentations and assuage his fears. He'd taught him how to read his own failures as being the essence of a precious chapter in the eternal adventure for knowledge. Fred was aware of his friend's bravado, but he had never gotten to know him well enough to imagine him alone with his suddenly-silenced phantoms, beyond the noise that he provoked willingly around himself in the desperate spreading of hopes and illusions under the most bizarre pretexts.

"We're not meant for deeds, but for ideas. *To think* means infinitely more than *to do*. Any idiot can do something at the end of the day, which doesn't mean he can change things or leave a trace... In the head, here," Sam tapped his bald scalp with his long and bony amateur-pianist's fingers, "here is where everything happens, everything starts and ends right here. Other than that, it's only confusion. The masses need to be fooled to keep the mechanism moving," Sam smiled hopelessly, feigning contentment.

"I should have left books behind me. Books. That's my destiny," murmured Fred, filling his pipe in order to keep his glance lowered. "And since I came over here, what have I written? Not a single book, nothing."

"You wrote them, but you wrote them in your head. It's the same. Even better. They're not dated, dusty, anachronistic. You can modify or save them whenever you want. What's the spoken or written word?"

spouted Sam with his eyes closed, overwhelmed by his own spontaneity. "Finite energy, consumed, dead. Once it's been let loose, the word submits to these outside laws, allows itself to be interpreted, perverted, manipulated, vulgarized, slaughtered… And I don't even know what's worse—for it to be understood and therefore loose its mystery, or not to be understood and become a weapon in the hands of madmen. In either case, the word's force is limited if it's uttered or written. The uttered word goes to the heavens or hell knows where; the written word lies in agony on library shelves or on the bookshelf of some hairdresser who reaches for it instead of taking a sleeping pill. We don't want this, do we? We don't care for confrontation or other mediocre displays of worthless pride, and immortality doesn't preoccupy us either. But truth does. Or the truth will stay well-hidden in its egg, well cared for by unseen forces, those superior entities that control all things, leaving the chain just long enough for us not to go insane if we come too close to it. In essence, this world is led as it is." Sam made wide gestures with his arms in the air, through the maintenance of limits.

And when he said this he clutched and twisted his fists as if he were about to strangle a pigeon:

"Limits! Think about this. Without them we'd be immortal but still the slaves of chaos, free but the prey of universal disorder. And what is our purpose in this life? To destroy our limits, to conquer them, to dissolve ourselves under the pretext of evolution and progress.

Thankfully, our subconscious is more intelligent than our consciousness; it shields us from useless heroic acts (and destructive ones, too), and it places barriers in the unconscious path of the destruction of limits. How else could you explain failure, fucking up, giving up, illusory joy, diseases, death... Everything is too spick-and-span. An admirably conceived insurance system. There is no salvation."

Sam was a brilliant analyst of nothings with pretenses to grandeur, a hysteric who drew water from a stone and softened the hardest metal with his voluptuous tones, a choleric who functioned on vodka, exaggerations and speculations, like a utopian system that longed to convince itself of its own legitimacy.

He'd been born in Prague, his father a banker, prudent and thrifty, much older than his beautiful and airy mother, an amateur photographer (although she could have been a model), gifted with much artistic sense that would later become common sense. His father, who had ensured them a leisurely existence, died when Sam was 12, after which his mother took him to Israel, where she would have relationships with three men, each older than the last and better off, all of whom died just on time, leaving her whatever they had.

After the death of his first stepfather, Sam had enough resources to come to America. He earned a PhD in art history at Columbia University and married a Protestant five years his senior, the sort of serious woman for whom marriage was an aim, the means to save herself from the pressure of finding a career. A professorship at a college in Ohio came Sam's way, not exactly a glorious prospect for one who had been taken in by the cosmopolitanism of large cities, their devouring energy with which he put up with his own neurosis. He mixed in with the anonymity of the melting pot, joyfully rummaging through its depths, fascinated by the idea of the emigrant's identity, redefining himself in his middle age, when native residents count their earnings and enjoy their pensions and life-long savings, shielded from the problems of those who belong to two worlds—or more, as in his case. Hence his friendship with Fred, another wanderer among cultures in search of the golden fleece.

Sam moved to Ohio, where only Fanny felt at home, finally in control of a tiny and well-regulated universe. For her, New York had always been a useless appendix that held onto Long Island, where she'd been born and where she'd never left until she met Sam. Even her collegiate experience was limited to Stony Brook, half an hour from home. She went to Manhattan once a year, during the winter holidays, to see the tree at Rockefeller Center. And if she hadn't bumped against Sam one of those winters in the swinging door of a café on Madison Avenue, spilling her hot coffee on his white pants, she would still be living in Long Island.

"What can I do? Fanny is part of my destiny," Sam excused himself. "I think it was the only time in her life when she bought a cup of coffee on Madison Avenue.

Her naiveté endeared me to her, the way in which she rolled her eyes, longing to be expressive; the ease with which she revealed her provincialism; the fact that she seemed to be who she was. I thought that I could shape this loud, yet older hen, and this drew me to her! But, as opposed to your Mimi, she stubbornly resisted everything. When she became a wife, she wanted nothing else. For a while, her care for me flattered me. I would have given her many children, which she'd wished for since I'd met her. In time, she became a sort of *stand-by soul*—how can I put it—you can't leave it or put it aside, for a sort of affection intervenes, pity…"

Fanny hadn't been able to have children, and Sam had opposed her insistence to adopt a child from a third-world country, so they got old together, she bored and he indifferent to her periodic criticism. When youth gave the first signs of fading, Fanny could no longer keep up with her cynical husband's humor, the flexibility of his mind rummaging hungrily through places that were inaccessible to her, so she abandoned her alertness to an apathy that she kept up in Ohio through eating sweets, playing card games and singing in the church choir.

Fifteen years prior, Sam had found himself the heir of a two-room apartment in Manhattan, property left to him after the death of his third stepfather. His mother had convinced his stepfather that since he didn't have children, he could at least leave it to her son, who had struggled with the American Dream as a professor who was unenthusiastically enriching the middle class in one of the American states.

Sam took Fanny mostly by force and installed her in Midtown Manhattan, where she would never adapt— even less so than an emigrant who came to start over again would. The only good thing was that Fanny was close to her mother's again—a two-hour drive—so that weekly, or however often she felt like it, she went to Long Island, lunched in the back garden drinking cocktails and always chewing gum or something else, and declared herself relaxed finally, far from Sam's dreams. At his end, Sam prized his solitude becomingly.

In the year that he received his inheritance and decided that he would move back to Manhattan, Sam was diagnosed with multiple sclerosis. The disease began violently, with severe episodes that had persuaded the doctors to sign off on his early retirement.

"How things fall into place! I told you, everything comes from here," Sam had said, tapping his bald head theatrically. "You'd think that I caused my disease to get rid of work and that stupid provincial place. But I have no desire to give in. With all these horrible health crises, I feel that I've only come to life now. I still have things to do here. To understand something, to sabotage a bit of what everyone thinks they've understood. To perfect my philosophical system... In the end, now I have time, and New York is perfect for my research. What more could I wish for? And I'm more inspired than ever. Now I realize how much the years teaching drained me, how much time I wasted with those students, robots without any interest beyond the dreams of their career and the mall, where all their upbringing and their general culture come from."

That day something was different. Fred stroked his beard slowly, as he did whenever he evaluated a situation. He lay before Sam on the edge of the couch and almost wished to caress his head. For the first time, Sam seemed shorter and unhappier than he was.

"What's wrong with you?" Fred asked.

"My mother died. They called me last night from Israel," answered Sam, and he extended his long greyhound neck, keeping still with his hands on his knees.

"And will you go to the funeral?"

"How do you want me to get there? Israel's the end of the world," Sam shook his head like a pendulum. "And my legs are weaker now. The Filipino nurse that cared for her told me that her burial is tomorrow. She'll take care of everything. Mother left her some things."

The image of a defeated Sam sitting on his little red chair troubled Fred. His headache returned with a vengeance. He came at a wrong time, but that was that!

"I'm very sorry. May God rest her in peace. How old was she?"

"Ninety-six. And perfectly healthy."

"Yes, nowadays people die healthy."

"Drink a shot of vodka and leave this be," murmured Sam, oscillating between sadness and the temptation to converse about his favorite subject, death, a fat and interminable worm.

"But I notice that you're really sitting Shiva." Fred motioned with his head toward the seat on which Sam squatted in his shorts, like a deformed child who had been punished and was made to torment himself even more.

"Of course, I'm sitting Shiva. But what I really should do is sit on the floor for seven days."

"Better than on that chair."

"What's bad about this chair?"

"I don't know. It's silly. Where did you find it?"

"The cat sits on it."

"And you think what you're doing is good?"

"Fred, look, here is the deal," replied Sam after a long sigh. "Forget the details. I'll order something from the Turkish restaurant across the street. I'm going to the synagogue."

"Now?" Fred frowned disappointed. "Since when do you go to synagogue?"

"I must. You understand. I'll be back in less than half an hour. It's the evening prayer; I need to go at least tonight. But relax! Women can also go to this synagogue; we count them too, so we are at least ten altogether and the prayer goes smoothly. Wait for the food; I'll be back in no time."

"I don't want to be left here alone."

"Why?" Sam elongated the "y" as he tied his right shoelace as tightly as possible. It was the one that always became undone.

"I'm tired of loneliness."

"Eh, I hadn't expected to hear this. Are you going crazy?"

"Why do you think I've gone crazy?" Fred jumped up excitedly. "Crazy are these writers you are reading now! How can you like this type of literature? Yes, *that* is insane. Malmeev and Sorokin too. The Russians went mad. But don't you say I went crazy, you hear me! I can't bear to hear that word."

As he spoke, Fred's face contorted and he felt his blood pulse in his temples and burn his eyes. He never got angry, couldn't remember the last time he was angry; his powerless revolt could only soften his muscles. He spoke slowly, but softly, his voice falling down into his body. There was the real cry; there it seethed inside him, smoldering in flesh and nerves. Sam glanced at him indifferently.

"Are you in a blue mood? Since when is loneliness bad for you? Isn't it one of our most valuable goods?" smiled Sam, pushing his kippah to the tip of his head. "Didn't we fight for it and sacrifice everything for it—anyway, everything that is useless in our lives, it's true, but those are still sacrifices, right? Women, children, children, women, jobs, money: a waste of time in this world where thousands of books and ideas will remain unknown to us or, even worse, they will survive us. It's not easy to become an uncomfortable cynic, a sophisticated arrogant person, an elitist snob, superior and freed from conventions. We've worked some, wouldn't you say? Cynicism needs to be cultivated, arrogance maintained. Those around us should be made to submit to their own limits and kept at a distance. What greater triumph is there than to be misunderstood and detested? At least this culture is good for that—at isolating you, making you lonely, dehumanizing you—God, how wonderful it sounds!"

"And you sound like those writers that you get intoxicated with nowadays. Don't pull me into that sinking boat. My purpose was never to destroy anything around me, but to build something solid within me. I wanted to get close to essences, you understand, because I know how dangerous it is to get close to the truth. And I can't expose anyone dear to me to this ultimately destructive experience. I chose loneliness not as a form of domination, nor self-flagellation; it was the only way to survive this hell somehow. Did I mess up? Perhaps. But don't associate me with your elitist speculations from where you pull your false energies and the venom of your ideas. I'm not at all for this sort of sectarian resistance through culture."

"Resistance? Quite the opposite, my dear. We're talking about capitulation. We chose to give up before we started fighting. We satisfied ourselves with studying techniques, tactics, strategies, methods; we showed those communists what a true battle should look like, and then we climbed the tower to see how they slaughtered one another. Or how they disembowel themselves. We showed them the way; it's enough. Who says we have to follow the same way ourselves?"

"Stop it, Sam! You'd better go to synagogue. Your theories sicken me."

"Don't act crazy!"

"I'm not crazy," sighed Fred, and his voice lowered again. He looked at Sam fearfully. "I'm not crazy," he repeated, avoiding looking him in the eye, staring instead, by instinct, at the surreal painting on the wall, to hide his embarrassment. "Chosen loneliness is one thing; imposed loneliness drives me nuts. You don't have time for me now that you're so involved in prayer and synagogue!"

"My mother died, Fred."

"That's precisely why what you do doesn't matter."

"Fred, with the death of the mother, something perishes inside us. The chaos where reference points no longer exist begins to come forth. A large part of our soul has been amputated. We're orphans. It doesn't matter what our age is when it happens. The umbilical cord gets cut again, this time an invisible one, the unseen link to the original matrix. There's no one left to be happy for us or worry for us; we have no one to prove to us who we are; no one cares what will become of us."

"Strange, but my relationship to my mother became stronger only after I left her. To leave your mother and your country, your language, yes, these separations have something in common. We, emigrants, know this. We're like seeds yanked from a protective fruit by the wind, too tired to grow again in other soil."

"Strange, this mix in you of depth and pathos. Some call it sensibility. But it's not worth the paper it's written on if there's no intelligence to back it up. You're a true artist, Fred, and this is where everything comes from. We'll have to talk about this again."

Suddenly, Sam got up from his seat, which he'd seemed glued to. He put a pair of pants on, went around the large mirror covered by a bed sheet, placed a bottle of vodka on the table and pinched off a piece of cheddar from the refrigerator. He glanced at Fred.

"Go on and have a drink. In the Talmud it says that you shouldn't enjoy anything for a month after a parent's death, so I'll drink from pain when I return. Coerced. As for the other pleasures, I don't think the Talmud refers to the wife," Sam wanted to smile, but the bone ache that tormented him daily merely made him grimace. "It's good that she went to her mother's over the weekend. They're both eating cookies, filling themselves up and talking nonsense about me. Wait for me, we'll talk when I return about what's troubling you now. Sam's booth is open until late at night. What did you say the matter is? Ah, yes, loneliness... dear loneliness! I can't wait to write an ode to it. God has destined us for great riches!"

How could he have known that these would be the last words Sam would speak? They took him straight from the synagogue to the emergency room. They tried everything they could and then took him to the morgue with a tiny white plaque tied to the toe of his left foot, where his name, the diagnosis of 'cerebral hemorrhage' and the hour of his death were written.

Fred waited for him until late, suspecting nothing. Sam's cat, black as coal, old and fat, had begun to fidget, running through the house excitedly, then went back, climbed up the red chair and meowed harrowingly. Overwhelmed by his headache, realizing he didn't have his medicine with him, Fred decided not to wait for Sam anymore. He could postpone the discussion till the following day. He left, adjusting the latch so it locked and slamming the door behind him.

When he got home, Mimi was still out. He didn't even get a chance to turn on the light when his telephone vibrated in his chest pocket. It was Fanny. He heard her mumbling something between hiccups of tears. She wanted to tell him something, but she could only guffaw incoherently. Bad news has something surreal about it. The delivery starts loudly and falls into opaque silence. Time and reason stop for several moments, life is cut from the known way of things and tied to a new one. The shock that follows the news, good or bad, comes from an effort to understand the modification of reality, to accept the turning upside down of the order and the recalibration of one's inner wheels for a different world with new rules.

Fred knew all of this, had written about it, but nothing exists until it happens to oneself. He remained paralyzed in the darkness until Mimi came home.

Tenderly, she helped him get his clothes off and go to bed. She covered him with two blankets, but his body continued to shake, and she held him in her arms like a child until morning.

4.

IT WAS A STIFLING SUMMER. MIST CAME out of the blacktop; air conditioners whirred in windows; New York had become a cement box where humidity greased people and walls. From the window, Central Park seemed a green heart chiseled in time. Outside, on the streets, the unbearable smell of horse urine awaited tourists in front of the Plaza.

Fred hadn't left the house in several days. He'd finished his book, which stood piled up on the rosewood desk in the living room, which two years earlier, Mimi had ordered for his birthday from an expensive antique shop. Jim had counseled him to publish the novel in Romania, where he was famous and people were anxious to see his newest book, which he had written after emigrating to the New World.

"There's no point in waiting. The translation might take longer than you think, and even if well-translated—by some miracle, since I doubt there are many American-born people who speak Romanian fluently—it's not certain that we'll find a publisher who'll want to publish it. Not unless you're Chekhov, anyhow. These folks bet on the celebrated dead and don't involve themselves with the living, except for foreign celebrities," smirked Jim, exhibiting his well-delivered cruelty during moments of humor. "Anyway, you could also hit the jackpot. I was hoping for that for years, too. The publishing world might adopt you if you're a genius, after which it swallows you and that's it. You're not your own self anymore; you belong to the industry of success. You understand how it is? It's bad, in any case. You'll have insomnia either way if you're a real artist. Some drown themselves in alcohol, others take drugs, and all take anti-depressants. Obsessions remain obsessions. These never pass; that's why they're obsessions. And if you're successful, anxiety grows; the fear of losing it all presses down on you. You're on top now, yes, but every tip is also the edge of an abyss. A moment of distraction, a wrong move and you're done for. As for me, thank God I saved myself on time!"

Mimi had gone to a reception, and Fred sank, as usual, into his brown leather couch, his lifeboat, from which he didn't know how and when he'd get out. He lit his pipe and fixed his gaze on the wall in front of him, a Le Clezio book unopened on his knees.

They had lived for years in that spacious condo on Central Park West and he still didn't feel at home there. Too few doors and too many windows. He came from a world full of walls through which any crack, no matter how small, brought a bit of oxygen inside. If you stuck your head out for a bit, the strong air of freedom would make you dizzy. Here, air was finely measured, conditioned, regulated. Windows didn't even need to open, so to speak. The concept of clean air, which had made such a stir before, was gone.

Mimi had decorated the apartment with the help of an architect and a designer, to make it just perfect now that she was rich. She got rid of some walls, so that the kitchen, living room and dining room opened up to form a huge and spectacular room for guests, though one lacking intimacy. Fred had taken refuge in his studio, having agreed to Mimi's tastes—somewhat pretentious and bourgeois—but with which he'd made his peace in the end and in which he'd been able to find a warm corner in the armchair placed near the window. The room was full of bookshelves, and Fred knew where to find each book without fail.

When everything seemed finished and the last candle had been placed on the edge of the bathtub by a long vase with tiny white stones on the bottom—it was like a swan's neck, three bamboo shoots having planted themselves into it—Mimi suddenly announced a surprise to him: the Steinway piano was to arrive. It would not only ennoble their salon, but it would give him a chance to play again.

"I haven't played since I was twelve."

"It's time to pick it up again. You'll see how well you feel," Mimi prophesied. "And it's good for parties. I told everyone you're the Renaissance man type. Art, literature, philosophy, music. It makes a great impression here."

"I can't stand dilettantism or improvisation. As for fashionable bragging, I don't remember. I don't play the piano, understand that—not at parties and not alone. I hate belaboring foreign languages, the mutilation of arts and any manner of imperfections, and that would be my piano playing," he said with a harsh voice.

He went to his studio and slammed the door behind him to make his point.

Mimi shrugged her shoulders and left him alone, but she brought in the piano, which seemed to her an essential part of the decor, and put two crystal candlesticks on it.

Three weeks later, she gave a party (with champagne and caviar) to inaugurate the new home; her business partners were the invitees. Fred was silent and polite, and Mimi was "dazzling," as Sheppard whispered into her ear while arranging one of her blonde locks, intentionally left to look rebellious.

After her guests' departure, Mimi, a bit dizzy from the combination of champagne and happiness, put on some jazz music in the background and moved the two candlesticks on the table, picked up her skirt and sat on the piano—which she'd probably seen someone do in some film—and wrapped her legs around Fred's thighs. Fred let her unbutton his pants and caressed, licked and bit, and penetrated her quietly while she let out thin and high-pitched cries of pleasure, like a soprano practicing her aria without an orchestra.

In the years that followed the blessing of the house on the piano—as Mimi had titled her well-directed erotic moment—Fred spent his life mostly in the apartment, and Mimi outside of it. Sometimes he felt like a prisoner, sometimes a master in that space that he had gotten used to and had even come to like, but which lacked something to make him feel at home.

He tried to find the answer in Mimi's repeated absences, or in the forgotten manuscript on the desk, or in his mother's refusal to visit him in New York, or in the long summers, so different from those in Romania that had passed lightning-fast in between book launches in bookstores and full halls where he was awaited, listened to, admired by readers and elegized by the literary critics. Here, summer was a lazy octopus floating on stagnant water.

Mimi came back beaming, like any person grateful not only for a beautiful summer, but also for a good season for business. She slammed all the doors in her path, lit all the candles, threw her shoes in the middle of the room, lowered the music and came straight to him.

"Why don't you listen to something else?"

"It's Brahms."

"It may well be, but it's depressing."

She was elegantly dressed or—better put— undressed with distinction. Fred's face livid in the light, suddenly blinding, and his quiet sadness vanquished her heart. She sat on the carpet by his legs. She took his hands in her own and stared him in the eye with admiration and wisdom, as she hadn't done since Paris, when she had still wanted to conquer him.

"What's missing inside your soul, my love?"

"I don't know," Fred answered calmly, as if it had been the most normal question between spouses that traveled on the same train, in the same compartment, facing each other but glancing in different directions. "I ask myself that too. I think it's nothing that you can give me or that I can have. The more I think about it, the less of a reason or solution I find."

Mimi waited. She had hoped that he'd be able to tell her more, to open up, to speak, to complain about her, to complain about something else, about anything. But Fred said little. He had spoken little all his life, and now his words were more precious and rare.

Another summer that would bring nothing.

Mimi pulled herself closer and placed her head on his knees.

"I'd like a child. I think that is what's missing for both of us. Now we don't have to worry about anything. My business is going great. We have money. Why not? I'll be 39 this year. If we don't have one now, good-bye motherhood. We can bring my aunt from Romania to take care of him, so you can see about your writing and I can grow my business. Didn't you say that in the Talmud it says that a man must do three things in this life: plant a tree, write a book and make a child?"

Fred ruminated in silence. After so many years in which she should have gotten to know him, Mimi still understood his words on a superficial level. She ignored reality when it pleased her. He didn't want to upset her, but as soon as she whispered the word "child," he saw a vague form folded in cloth, like Jesus from the nativity scene, which stores displayed on Christmas in their windows, as did churches and parks. A child?

"The thing is that for three years I haven't used any protection, and still never got pregnant. I had my blood tests two weeks ago. I'm OK. Everything's all right with me."

Fred was startled. It wasn't a spontaneous idea, then; this discourse was premeditated; she'd chosen her moment. There was no reason to resist it. Women do what they please, no matter what.

"The doctor also suggested that you get examined too. Pardon me for asking: have you ever gotten anyone pregnant?" Mimi asked rashly, hinting at his past in Romania, in his youth, before he met her.

Fred gulped and shook his head, feeling his Adam's apple as it bulged as if struggling to get out.

"Well, see? You need to get examined to see where we stand. Tuesday at 5:00 we're booked at the urologist's."

She kissed him hastily on a knee and went to the bathroom, changing Brahms to Bossanovas on her way. For once, Fred followed her.

"What do you mean *we* booked an appointment at the urologist's?"

"Fred, in this country people don't have inhibitions. I thought you understood this by now," cried Mimi through the open door while she brushed her teeth with an especially sharp brush that had a tiny red bird-like beak. "People are comfortable in their own skins, speak openly about their problems. They go around with their wives everywhere, they have nothing to hide," mumbled Mimi, spitting the water as gracefully as possible into the sink. "The doctor asked us both to come, but don't worry, you'll take the test in private, my love, by yourself. Here, over and above all, intimacy is respected."

Since she'd made it big, Mimi had become a grand defender of American society whose virtues she saw even in its failures.

Fred didn't shut an eye that night. Why had he given up so easily? A child crawling on his fours among stylish furniture, between Mimi or the piano's invincible legs, on which lately the dust alone would settle. And he wasn't sure that Mimi really wanted to become a mother, only that she wanted to enrich her track record with a child.

Toward the morning, Fred fell asleep, dreaming of a lake with blue water. In his dream, he felt an overpowering desire to swim, but lay fully clothed. He rolled his pant cuffs, but as soon as he went into the water, his legs froze. And the water was shallow; it hardly covered his ankles.

The urologist's office was dark and almost empty. A short examining table looked like a coffin for a dead person without legs. On a narrow table was a box from which the finger of a disposable plastic glove emerged.

On the wall hung a colored drawing of the urinary tract, two purple kidneys looking like beans tied around a round sack placed between the skeleton's legs. It was a drawing of a human body concentrated exclusively on the production and expulsion of urine. There was a small desk behind on which a urologist sat, looking even smaller than he was, wearing huge thick-framed glasses.

He and Mimi stood stiff before his desk. Mimi in a colorless suit, decent, almost sad from her point of view, and Fred with his coat buttoned till the last button, bluer and much more luminous than his eyes.

On the right wall they noticed another drawing—a cross section of a penis. Mimi analyzed it with an eye for science. Fred looked the other way. The doctor arranged his hair-piece, opened his file calmly and asked Fred how old he was, what diseases and surgeries he'd had, what pills he took, whether he had allergies, and checked something off every time Fred gave an answer.

"Can I ask you, on a scale of one to ten, what number would you give your erection?"

The question came calmly. Mimi perked up her ears, and Fred put his head down.

"Seven to eight," murmured Fred after a moment of silence.

"Six to seven," Mimi heard herself saying.

"Good," said the doctor, glancing at Mimi with a gratified smile.

"Come with me, sir," he said to Fred. "Your wife will wait here."

He took him into another room where the decor was much the same. A tiny nurse awaited him there. The urologist excused himself. Another patient was waiting for him, and the nurse smiled warmly and handed him a test tube.

"You've decided to do it here?"

"What do you mean?"

"You can do it here, or you can do it at home and bring us the sample. But it's better here. The fresher and warmer it is, the better."

Fred smiled back at her. He couldn't help but hold his tongue and show off his sense of humor. If it was better to do the test there, then he was better off doing it there—what was he waiting for?

"Do you need help?" the nurse asked him with professional care.

"Which would mean?" asked Fred amused.

"Would you like me to give you a magazine? Or maybe you'd like your wife to be with you?"

"Oh, no. I'll be fine by myself," said Fred, playing along.

"Very good. Lock the door behind you. When you're done, bring the sample to the adjoining room. There's no rush."

She smiled again, this time friendlier:

"You have a very beautiful shirt."

"Thank you," answered Fred, without knowing whether this compliment was part of the professional ritual meant to stimulate self-confidence.

"Good luck!" said the nurse, as if she expected him to pass an exam, climb a mountain or win the lottery.

Left alone, he locked the door. He opened his upper coat-button, inhaled and sat on the only chair in that small white austere room that looked like an antiseptic cell of a prison. He felt at ease, strangely well. A small window facing an interior wall was open, and the cooing of pigeons that had made their nests under a roof could be heard from outside. He took his wallet from his pocket and noted some ideas. Then his eyes fell on the tube that he had carefully placed on the narrow table, and Mimi's worried face suddenly came to his mind.

He imagined her nervously pacing up and down in the waiting room, her gait, making her legs shake when she was excited, like a pony unwearied of running and jumping. And Mimi's buttocks, humid in the morning, the pink partition wherein he slipped his palms as if in a fissure pulsing between two white and round volcanoes that exploded with vigor. He pulled the tube closer, but Mimi's ass lost itself in the color of the pale suit she was wearing that morning.

He ought to think about his schoolmate Gina, about her thick lips, so thick that they split easily. She always greased them with shiny ointment, provoking all sorts of fantasies in the 9th graders, ending in erections hidden beneath manuals or towels in the locker room.

Or his first love, Adela, the girl with the finest breasts in high school, as they had been unofficially declared by the Rumor Club, a group of educated, still unformed adolescents who pretended to be cynical to mask their repression. Fred saw her breasts after the 1st of May parade. The girls in the class were performing a number before the judges, forming the shape of the country, waving scarves colored like the national flag, and the boys wore placards with all sorts of portraits of Communist leaders. When the circus ended, all of them went to Herăstrău Park where they ate warm hot dogs and drank beer amid the girls' laughter.

Fred and Adela had gone away from the group to lie on the grass beneath willows on the edge of the lake. Adela had put her scarf beneath her so as not to get cold, and he had slipped his arm beneath her shoulders, and with his other hand, opened the buttons of her blouse and quietly caressed her winsome breasts until he felt the lake expand, about to cover them. Adela's breasts remained planted in his mind, stuck there like two white masts, flying the colors of the national flag which each time moved him when he saw it being raised at the Olympics.

He went through a long line of asses, breasts, thighs and lips, but the test tube remained empty and he felt all the better sealed in his white cage. He wrote down some things in his notebook. He felt thirsty, but it seemed that the reaction was foreseen—there were two tiny water bottles on the table and a package of plastic cups. This made him happy; it seemed his reactions were normal. Other detainees had had the same desires, the same needs; their throats, too, had gone dry from waiting, or from emotion, or from effort, or simply from loneliness.

He opened a drawer—left intentionally half-opened, perhaps—and came across a magazine with beautiful naked women standing in provocative positions. After the first page he took the tube in his hand and in the moment when a black bird landed on the windowsill with a chirp, he ejaculated quietly and professionally, as the tiny nurse with her complicit gaze had encouraged him to do.

"Why didn't you tell me you had the mumps?" complained Mimi when they received the results. "And you didn't tell the urologist either."

"It didn't seem important to me," Fred excused himself clumsily. "I thought it's just a superstition, not a medical explanation."

"Lord! We could have avoided all of this, and you wouldn't have had to go through those humiliating moments."

"They were very pleasant moments, Mimi. You don't need to worry."

"And aren't you thinking about me? I wanted a child," Mimi stomped her foot. "I needed a child."

"Anything is possible. A college friend who had the mumps at the same time left a regiment of women pregnant. It's all about not losing your hope. The mind can do much more than the body. It surpasses limits; it can turn verdicts upside down. And you can visualize and program the future, can't you?"

"I never know whether you're ironic, whether you're serious, or whether you're talking to me or just using phrases from your books," rattled Mimi in one breath, as if this had nagged at her soul for a long time.

"Because you don't read my books," he smiled without a trace of reproach as he stroked his chin, a reflexive defense mechanism beneath which he had hidden himself for years.

"But I know what they're about."

"What they're about matters least."

"I don't have time, Fred. You can see that I work all day."

"And those spiritual guides on the nightstand?"

"That's different. I need those."

"Professional literature?" insisted Fred, and he immediately regretted the maliciousness of the question.

"You can call it that," continued Mimi, holding her own, "but to tell you frankly, I don't really like reading your books. These manuscripts of yours seem provisional to me—I don't know how to put it—unfinished, coverless. I'll read it when it comes out at Barnes and Nobles, so I can be proud of you. Everyone asks me when that book that I've been talking about for years is coming out."

"I'm not exactly a winning horse, Mimi."

"You aren't *anymore*," Mimi corrected him, irritated.

"I never was. Other people thought I had virtues that were commensurate to their expectations. I run, that's it. I don't dream of winning. I don't care about it. I have too many things to do in this race course, anyway. I thought you understood. Otherwise, it seems that this time you made a poor bet," he told her calmly.

Mimi's expression changed, but she didn't offer a riposte.

"In any case, I don't appear in any of your books. You never wrote about me," said Mimi to bring the discussion back to her territory. "Painters paint their spouses, writers put them in books. You never considered me important enough to make a character out of me. And if you want to know, you might have been successful had you written about me."

"But I do write about you, Mimi, only that you refuse to recognize yourself."

Fred maintained his smile and took his pipe from his pocket, the last refuge of comfort.

"What do you mean?"

"Even if you don't appear like a simple character, as you expect, my writing is impregnated by you."

"At least you're writing, dear, since you could never impregnate me." Mimi returned his smile like a knife blade and put her purse over her shoulder, restless to end the discussion from her higher point. "I need to run. The accountant is waiting for me at the spa. What are you doing tonight? I'll be late. They have a special launch at *Dior*. I'm going with Jessica. Eat, don't wait for me. And if you leave, don't forget to put the alarm on."

He let her go and lay on his armchair feeling smaller, as she had seen him once. Even the shadow that the lamplight projected on the wall had gotten smaller. When he lit his pipe, he noticed for the first time that his hand trembled slightly.

After several months in which he had tried unsuccessfully to find a literary agent in New York, Fred received a letter from a publisher in Romania. They wanted to publish his novel, which the censorship had blocked in Romania, in a complete edition of his works. The contract was generous. For several weeks Fred said nothing to Mimi about the letter; neither did he hasten to answer it. He didn't care whether the book came out now or not. Books have their own time. Or authors have a temporal relationship to their works. They adore them when they're newborns and estrange themselves from them as they age.

The director of the most important publisher in Bucharest called him one morning, forcing him to allow publication and to promise that he'd go to the launch, no matter how much he wanted to avoid it.

In the end, he made his peace with the idea, mainly because it meant he'd see his mother again. She had always been brave and categorical when she said:

"Stay there. Take care of your life. You have nothing to do here. I have everything I need; it's enough for me to talk with you on the phone, to write and know you're healthy. I only want to see you happy and successful."

She never mentioned New York or America. This *there* was a vague territory in his mother's mind, without an identity. She was simply happy that her son had saved himself, that he'd found himself on the other side, outside of Romania, in a world where she thought he was going to reach the fame that his talent, of which she was so proud, deserved. She had a haughty pride. In the past weeks Fred had only spoken to her twice. She seemed tired, her voice was low, lacking energy. Or perhaps she was just aging.

Mimi forgot about the idea of having a child and signed up for a spirituality course. She went weekly to the Himalaya Center, where all sorts of people initiated in happiness and expert in matters of the soul strengthened her self-esteem and confidence, preparing her for success and immortality.

She came home like a bomb of energy and positivity; which Fred couldn't run away from. The excited explosion followed him to the bathroom as well:

"My love, you should come too. Your energy channels simply need to be opened up. You'll get in harmony with the universe, with superior entities. You were telling me about the super-ego. Well, I found that I'm almost there. I'm not joking. Everything is going my way. I've aligned my soul and mind. I feel the violet light of illumination flowing through me."

She would stack three or four bricks atop each other on a chair, take some steps back, and hurling herself with a warlike cry, break them in two. Then she'd triumphantly show her arms to Fred, her muscles still flexed.

"What do you say? I'm strengthening my will-power. I can defeat anything."

Fred tried to temper her unenthusiastically and unsuccessfully:

"Mimi, Mimi, you don't need muscles to get in touch with the super-ego or the unseen powers that they teach you about there. Ambition and stubbornness are primitive weapons. Silence is stronger than yelling. Between imagination and willpower, imagination always wins."

"I don't know what you're talking about. Why don't you do something with your imagination, then? I'm sick of all your words. In your mouth they seem more like obstacles than tools. I'm preparing to overcome obstacles, not to reflect on them."

Fred remembered how in the beginning of their relationship, she used to absorb his words, when she came home exhausted from the Parisian bar where she made crepes, thirsty to listen to him.

"I want to know everything. Everything. Teach me. I'm listening to you," Mimi would whisper and fall asleep in his then-strong arms, under his then-shining words able to tam the night.

Fred would caress her perfect, nude body and put her to sleep with stories about the ancient Greeks, read to her from Chekhov and Dostoevsky or tell her about the subconscious mind.

"We can imagine it a wise man who lives in our brain, like an old archivist who stores all the information, classifies our memories, records our every gesture, emotion, sensation, happening, and places it all in piles on shelves, building an infernally complex library in the inner spaces of our minds. This old archivist works stealthily in a dark room where every word and all sensations are numbered, arranged in an order and meaning that remain unknown to us, just as our brain has remained overwhelmingly unknown to us to this day."

Mimi would stretch languorously, lick one of his ears, nestle like a spoiled girl against his chest and ask him not to stop. And Fred would go on in the darkness, as if to himself:

"The subconscious is the subtle approximation of the conscious, the coefficient of error and equilibrium. It owns the entire portfolio and our whole heritage. It's the miracle-maker; it holds the ineffable under its key and can let good fortune loose. A troublesome old man, yet sometimes a brilliant conniver, ready to catch us in his trap or fool us with his tricks; other times he's a merry fairy pretending to be distracted, but sensitive to the unseen and to metaphors. We can speculate about his playful spirit, and we can provoke him to turn the rules of the game upside down. He's as much from our imagination as reality."

Mimi would snore softly and happily, simply and naturally, while Fred watched over this awed wonder in his arms. In the old days, he had also taught her how to defend her vulnerabilities and hide her strength. A way to save her femininity. That was in the beginning of their marriage, when she had assumed the status of a Pygmalion.

Their bedroom looked like a battlefield now. Weights, fitness balls, exercise bands and bricks. Deepak Chopra's books, tapes with relaxing music, new-age guides about how to achieve any goal in ten steps, how to become rich overnight, how to fight against stress and defeat your opponents in business, how to manifest your dreams and stop old age had made their way to the nightstand. Everything seemed so easy to reach. Mimi fell asleep in a trance, with her headphones on.

One day, she announced to Fred that she'd found her inner child.

"Long live he!" said Fred bored, and he decided to go to Romania to the launch of his book that once had been banned.

"It'll be a triumph," predicted Mimi. "Take pictures. Someone should film it. Record all of it. I want it all."

Her voice didn't have the tones of yesteryear and didn't convey any confidence. Her wish sounded like a commercial for toothpaste, or so it seemed to Fred.

"But my teeth are white, strong and beautiful, my dear," she said, as if answering Fred's silent thought. "With these teeth I fought and clawed for years to make things work for us, for you to now fly business-class back to the homeland, to show them all!"

Fred twisted his pipe between his fingers. He wasn't in the mood. He didn't want to show anyone anything. He had nothing to prove to anyone there. It was a closed chapter. More often than not, the epilogue is a pathetic appendix.

He convinced himself he went mostly to see his mother, to get away, to study how much nostalgia he still had for the place, how much frustration, how much curiosity for the changes he'd heard about. He hadn't been there in fifteen years, since he'd left for Paris, not because he'd been persecuted politically but because of pride, as revenge that his novel had been banned. A childish reaction, a vague motivation.

"I'd go to Bucharest with you," Mimi said to him, halfheartedly, "but my business is more important, my dear. It pays for our needs and pleasures. And I'd be second fiddle to you there. I don't know the literary world, and your mother will take over the whole scene, I'm sure. Go and savor your triumph."

"Enough of this triumphalism! It's not a victory. I return defeated."

"Defeated? Already? Have you given up?"

"Given up on what? Sometimes I wonder whether naiveté is a genuine state, a weakness or an evil."

"Are you talking about *my* naiveté?" Mimi laughed ironically, her hands clenching her hips.

"No, I mean generally. Naiveté as a service door. You can slip outside unobserved. A form of avoiding saying things directly, of involving yourself."

"Leave it alone, Fred. Your speculations annoy me. How would you like me to involve myself? I pay for everything; isn't that enough?"

"When I said that I return there defeated, I was thinking about my dilemmas, my uncertainty, which I haven't been able to get rid of. I still don't know whether I've done the right thing or where my place is."

"Your whole life will pass before you find an answer to those problems."

"Very possible."

"Your place is here. By me," whispered Mimi suddenly affected. "You are like a fresh spring, and I hold the banks steady for your smooth flow. Why don't you want to try something like meditation or yoga? It would help, you know. It's like someone pulls the wool off your eyes. Promise me that you won't let these thoughts eat you up. Please! I want you to be happy, to be at peace."

She knew how to ingratiate herself. Fred closed his eyes tenderly and pulled her closer. He embraced her and kissed her earlobe.

"I promise."

They lay glued to each other. Fred didn't try more. Her body vibrated. But he wasn't sure whether it vibrated from desire or from impatience. Mimi picked up a bit of fluff from his shirt, slipped from his arms as elegantly as possible and went to the bedroom to recite the mantra that she'd learned at the last meditation session.

The day Mimi left for a week to a spiritual center in upstate New York, Fred took a taxi to Kennedy Airport.

The taxi drove through Queens, close to Forest Hills, where he'd visited Anita years back. It was rumored that she'd lived with her agent who was younger than her by 24 years, whom she had chosen as her beneficiary. She'd invited Fred to her last retrospective at a Chelsea gallery, but Mimi was categorically against it:

"I don't want you to go. And I don't like her paintings. I'll never understand how this old witch can fool the entire world. Oh, and she has the nose of an English horn."

Several months after the exhibition, Anita had cardiac arrest. *The New York Times* dedicated half a page to her, published her photograph, her biography romanticized in the American style, and reproduced three of her works. The surprise came two weeks later, in a huge well-wrapped package in a wooden box dropped off by their apartment door.

Mimi was preparing for one of her evenings with her business partners and high-end clients. She'd ordered crates with champagne, boxes of caviar and goose liver and French cheeses. The porter called relentlessly as the parcels arrived. Mimi ordered him not to call her every time, rather to take them in and bring them upstairs. Fred heard her screaming:

"For God's sake, what's with this coffin?"

Inside was a note from the executor of Anita's last will and testament glued to one of her best-received paintings—the one Fred had liked when he'd visited her studio. It showed physical shadows larger than ethereal bodies, an exchange of energy, a reverse flow.

On the back was written: *Welcome to the feast of champions, Fred. Feast on New York, the most extravagant banquet. Remain ever curious, hungry and insatiable. Warmest wishes, Anita.*

"Hmm," grimaced Mimi. "What sort of wish is this? I'll put it in the closet in the basement. I don't want it here!"

When she found out how much the painting was worth, she immediately hung it up on the wall behind the piano and started showing it off to guests, explaining to them:

"A great painter. You've heard of her, of course. There were stories about her in *The New York Times*, she's sold at Sotheby's and was a good friend of ours. She wanted to be with us even after death."

Fred stared at her embarrassed while Mimi winked at him. Everyone liked the painting.

He couldn't sleep on the plane, despite having swallowed an *Ambien* and three glasses of whiskey.

At Otopeni Airport, a driver sent by the publisher awaited him. He was a short, tanned man with a sign on which the director had simply written "FRED" with a black marker. He measured Fred for a long time with his glance, greeted him hurriedly and told him to follow him to the car. He paid for the parking, opened the trunk and asked him if the flight had had any turbulence.

"Very little, over Labrador," answered Fred automatically, and he immediately felt silly. The driver had no reaction, as if he were used to flying weekly over Labrador.

Dinu would become his best friend during his Bucharest sojourn. He'd been a driver for all sorts of companies for over 25 years. He'd moved on from the political party structure to the post-revolutionary private sector without too much trouble. Quiet as a fish before the fall of communism and alert as a bird of prey after.

As soon as he got into the car, Fred instinctively tried to put on his seatbelt, but it was stuck to the backseat. Dinu stopped him, touching his arm gently.

"Leave it be. You're with me. You don't need it."

"I thought they give you a fine if…"

"To me? Who? These crooks? Don't you know what country we live in?"

Fred smiled. Dinu sped down the road, as if he had to win a race.

"It's an automatic movement for me," Fred excused himself, his hand still on the seatbelt.

"I figured. How long since you've been here?"

"Twenty years."

"Be careful when you take a cab. They'll smell you immediately."

Fred didn't ask anything after that. The road from the airport was nothing like what he remembered: company headquarters, advertisements and banners, expensive cars, new gas stations. He stared in silence. Dinu felt him out.

"Eh? Much has changed, right? But it's gone backward!"

When they entered the city, he had the feeling that he had left yesterday. Only that the traffic was heavy, the boulevards were crowded, and people drove bumper to bumper. Dinu mumbled quietly, as a guide embarrassed, as he would have liked to present another reality to the tourist next to him. When they passed a church, Dinu took his hands off the steering wheel and energetically crossed himself.

Skeletons of apartment buildings begun in Ceaușescu's time and abandoned since then appeared at certain intersections like the ghosts of a world that still struggled to wane. On Ana Ipătescu Boulevard, which had been renamed Lascăr Catargiu, old renovated mansions alternated with those left to crumble, whose plaster fell to ruins and where weeds had made their way through walls and roofs.

"Things would go better if we didn't have these politicians," Dinu said to him coolly, showing him a huge billboard with the portrait of a party leader and two sleeping dogs under the billboard. "We'll never get rid of our corruption and poverty. We don't have roads, either. Look, sir: we sit more than we move in traffic. But there's three times as many cars now."

"Big changes can't happen in one or two decades. Mentalities take more time to change than infrastructures."

"Woe to us! We got loads of new banks, casinos and nightclubs. The only thing that does well for itself is the private small business. As for the underground one, don't get me started."

"On a historical scale, it means nothing."

"Well, we don't matter at all either."

"In an absolute sense, it's true."

"Why don't you take off your jacket?" asked Dinu, noticing Fred had gotten agitated, his forehead sweating. "I can turn on the air conditioning, if you want. Though I hate it. It makes my left shoulder go numb."

He would rather have changed the subject. But Fred didn't want to talk at all.

They went on Magheru Boulevard, bumper to bumper all the way. It looked mostly the same, only it was now called Queen Elisabeta and office buildings had popped up, walls full of graffiti, casinos, sex shops. The Nottara Theater was still there, just as stale.

"The Scala bakery was here?" Fred felt himself saying it with an emptiness growing in his stomach.

"It was. It was destroyed a long time ago, during the earthquake. I don't remember whether it was where you now see the KFC or the Vodafone sign," said Dinu cheerfully, showing him two cellphones on the dashboard. "We all have two: one with an *Orange*, the other with a *Vodafone* calling card. We're always on a network. My cousin in the countryside has an outhouse, but he still has two cellphones."

"And the Cinema *Patria*?" asked Fred with a lighter voice.

"Gone. It's a travel agency now. Folks travel. They go to Paris or Venice on the weekends. Or to Milan, for shopping. They spend New Year's in Thailand. The upper class goes to Vienna. Eh, we live alongside them," Dinu added waggishly.

Fred heard without understanding. He was and wasn't there, sinking deeper and deeper in the passenger's seat.

When they entered the Cotroceni residential quarter, he took off his jacket. It was the street of his youth. Time seemed to have had no power there. The same old lindens, the same cracks in the blacktop. Only now, ultra-expensive cars were parked on the sidewalks. His neighbor's home had the same curtains—white, with rose garlands that he had seen for years on end. He felt nothing. His mother doubtlessly fervently awaited him after so many years. His childhood room. Everything seemed far away and cold.

Dinu turned the engine off, got out and brought the two suitcases onto the sidewalk in front of a forged metal gate. He gave Fred a business card and told him with a smile:

"I'm at your service. The director told me you should call whenever you need me. I'll come to take you at 11:00 AM tomorrow. He's waiting for you at the publishing house—so he told me."

Fred stared as his luggage as if it weren't his.

"Don't ignore premonitions, Fred," Mimi had once said to him. "They're our protective system. If you feel a nail in your chest, it's a bad sign and you should run! If you feel that you're growing wings, it's good."

"Do you want me to help you with the luggage? To take it inside?" Dinu asked.

"No, thank you," said Fred.

He put on his jacket and stared Dinu in the eye for the first time. A claw seemed to grab at his chest. A dog he didn't remember barked loudly in a neighbor's yard. The linden smell was dizzying.

"What time is it?"

"17."

"17?"

"Five in the afternoon here," said Dinu. "Are you tired?"

"Not at all. Would you like to take me somewhere?"

"Now?"

"Yes. Now."

"I'll take you, but isn't your mother waiting for you? That's what the director said: take him from the airport straight to his home, since he hasn't seen his mother in 20 years."

"I feel the need to delay that moment."

"Emotions?" Dinu smiled understandingly.

"Curiosity. Can you take me to the Animafilm Studio? And toward Herăstrău, then to The Nightingale's Park?"

Dinu frowned. He spoke to him slowly, as if speaking to a child who can hardly understand:

"I can. That's not the problem. But you see, it's rush hour now. The streets are crowded; you've seen it yourself. It'll take us two hours, or God knows how long. And Animafilm has closed. The Nightingales' Park is wasting away; the restaurant is abandoned. You don't know how it is around here. Things are different."

The edge of a curtain was drawn across his child-hood room window, and his aunt's head showed through. As soon as she saw him her hands grew agitated. She opened the window and cried:

"Come inside. The gate is open! We're waiting for you. Dinner is on the table!"

Dinu hastened to take the luggage into the yard, so Fred wouldn't change his mind. Fred waved to his aunt, opened the gate that squeaked just as in the old days, and with lowered shoulders, followed Dinu who threw the luggage on the stairs, hurriedly called to him:

"May you live long!" and jumped into the car, leaving quickly, wheels screeching, ready for a new battle.

Fred was glad that his aunt, four years younger than his mother, was there. The reunion would be easier. It was dark in the hallway which reeked of mold and pickled cabbage.

"Welcome!" His aunt kissed him on both cheeks and immediately ordered him to take off his jacket: "It's hot in here because the oven's been on all day! You look so good!"

She spoke hastily, barely giving him a good look. Fred didn't seem surprised that his mother didn't greet him at the door. She was sensitive and emotional; she probably wanted to avoid a difficult, weepy or loud reunion. She was delicate, with a common sense of situations. A claw gnawed at his chest again.

"Where is Mother?"

"In the living room. Where should she be?" answered his aunt quickly.

Then she grabbed his arm, propped him against the wall, put her arm against him and whispered hurriedly, swallowing her words and breathing heavily, as if she'd just climbed a mountain.

"Fred, I didn't want to tell you earlier. Anyhow, you couldn't do anything about it from over there. No one can do anything. Eva, poor her…"

"What's wrong with her? What happened?"

A hoarse, angry voice yelled from the adjoining room:

"Is no one coming to change this child? Where have you all gone?"

"Who else is here?"

The claw had clenched its way to Fred's heart.

"It's Eva, Fred. Eva. O, Lord! Wait a little bit… Listen to me. She's been like this for several months. Doctors say it's dementia. I moved in here to help her. I would have told you, but I didn't want you to worry, and I knew you'd come. Better this way. Don't get scared. She's calm. Sometimes she's even coherent and present."

He wanted to stop time and freeze up right there, in that dark hallway; then slowly melt into the walls. Instead, he went straight into the dining room. His mother was sitting at the table, nicely dressed, her hair combed. Just as he'd remembered her. But it wasn't her. To the right of her plate was a tiny stuffed bear, the tiny bear that he'd slept with since he was a child. To the left, a heap of cut-outs from a newspaper. On the lapel of her suit, a fresh food stain. His mother raised her eyes, smiled widely and said:

"Come on, the *sarmale* are getting cold. Where have you been till now?"

From that very moment, the week spent in Bucharest became a living nightmare. His aunt told him that doctors talked about his mother's long-term depression. Her answer to all of Fred's questions was the same: there's nothing we can do about it.

It was most painful to look at her. Her melancholic blue eyes that he remembered so well, were now opaque and empty. They looked through him, staring at an object and not moving for minutes on end. She had lost a lot of weight. Her clothes were loose on her emaciated body. Sometimes she made uncontrollable movements. Her voice had become deeper; everything irritated her, but she didn't have the strength to say more than a few words. She spent her days cutting newspaper articles. She'd told her sister that she'd gather everything that had been published about Fred. But she couldn't read anymore. And very little had been written about Fred since his return to the country. She would cut out photos and advertisements, pile them on the table, and start over the next day.

The meeting with his publisher was somber and felt like mere protocol. The publisher welcomed Fred jovially, introduced several young editors to him—they had certainly not read him—and offered him coffee and plain water with lemon, which Fred didn't touch. He told him in a casual tone that his novel would only get published with a print run of several hundred copies. There was no interest in Romanian writers; books are expensive and sell with difficulty; people struggle to survive, and between a pound of meat and a book there is no contest. What's more, people had forgotten him. It wasn't how Fred imagined it would be. Things had changed since he left. Values had shifted, and publishers were forced to apply hard economics to their businesses, as they did in the West. Fred should know all that well. The publisher didn't excuse himself; he just informed Fred and assured him that the following day his wife would come to the book launch.

"She used to read all of your books before the revolution. She was a great fan of yours."

It felt as if he didn't exist in the present, as if he'd returned from the dead for a week to the fatherland, which was going down a new road, having gotten rid of all uselessness. With that, the best years of his youth were lost too: vigor and first love, lectures and curiosity. Everyone spoke about *Before* and *After* the Fall, as about an apocalypse that had cut time in two. His countrymen counted their money by the millions and smiled superciliously whenever an intruder like him tried to pick up where he had left off, and tried to find the reference points of *Before* in the world of *Now*, a code only the locals understood.

"You never checked in in all these years, anyway," the publisher reproached him. "If you're not here to appear on TV, to give interviews, to affiliate yourself with influential literary groups, eh… Literary criticism needs to be oiled, too. The reader needs to be kept awake. People forget. And this new generation is quick. They have other idols."

The bookstore's window displayed his youthful portrait, surrounded by several copies of his recent novel. A fashionable literary critic who hadn't arrived yet would introduce him. His mother was in the front row, holding the stuffed bear close to her chest, under his aunt's watchful gaze. The aunt was fanning herself with a huge paper fan.

"When does it start? I want it to start now!"

"Eva, please." His aunt calmed her down. "It'll start soon."

Fred stepped outside. He couldn't take it anymore. He stared at the street from the doorway, numb. He wanted to leave it all and take the first plane back home. Where was that home? He had just returned home. He couldn't sleep in his childhood bed, nor could he sleep in the king-sized bed that Mimi had bought in New York. There was no quiet, no peace anywhere.

He felt like a stranger everywhere. A stranger in this strange city, whose every corner he had known; a stranger in the city he had emigrated to, where he'd thought he would find himself a warm home, whose magic and traps he'd struggled to discover; a stranger to the mother who now caressed a stuffed bear; a stranger to Mimi, who broke bricks with her fist in the bedroom; a stranger to his books, which no one cared for anymore. Perhaps he had had no childhood. Perhaps not even his words were his anymore. His head hurt. A young woman with long giraffe-like legs and disheveled hair over bare shoulders bumped against him on her way into the bookstore.

"Pardon me," she whispered.

Fred jumped. She looked like Dana. He stared at her intensely. It was Dana. Perhaps she had not died. But how could it be her? She would have been over 55. The girl looked at him curiously and smiled confused.

"Did you come for the launch?" Fred heard himself ask.

"Launch? What launch?"

Fred pointed to the showcase with his large photo surrounded by his books.

"Oh, no," she answered quickly. "I came to buy a wedding card."

She hadn't recognized him. She made no connection between the man in the photo and the one standing anxious and insecure by the bookstore door.

The boulevard bustled with people. Some were tourists with knapsacks, women with bags, businesspeople in business attire speaking foreign languages, an old lady begging in front of a pharmacy, beautiful girls that, judging by their clothing, could either be students or prostitutes; the fizzling of endless cars flowing bumper to bumper; a continuous noise, a mysterious agitation as in any large, vibrant, diverse city.

He felt like lying down on the sidewalk between the hurried legs aimed in particular directions. But he had neither a purpose nor a direction. He was like a ship stuck onshore, a wreck that passersby glanced at curiously, trying to imagine how he had looked some time ago. *Before.*

Mimi called to wish him good luck. He didn't say anything, nothing about his mother's condition, nothing about how he was feeling. He assured her that everything was fine.

The literary critic who was supposed to present his book appeared in a hurry. He greeted Fred as if it had been mere days since their last meeting and excused himself for being late. The members at the editorial meeting of the magazine where he worked had told him nothing about the novel. Whether he liked it or not, he was simply doing his duty. He'd praise Fred, anyhow, that's why he was there. A young woman accompanied by a cameraman came up to Fred, handed him a microphone and said hastily:

"How wonderful that we caught you before it starts! We're from TVR International. Can you give us a few words, please? We can't stay for the launch."

There were only a few people in the bookstore. Some were writers, some old and bored ex-colleagues from Animafilm Studio, some folks who had chanced upon the launch by mistake, found themselves in the bookstore right then, and the publishing director and his wife, and Dinu smiling happily in the back row. The critic spoke for a long time, read fragments, scolded him for not maintaining a stronger connection to the fatherland. Fred uttered some tense thanks, avoiding looking at his mother. She didn't look his way, either.

He signed autographs on the few books that sold. A saleswoman put cookies and plastic glasses with wine on a table. The launch was done. The bookstore was soon empty. Each person went to his own business after congratulating Fred formally, shook his hand and patted him on the back. No one asked him what it was like over there, what it was like to be a writer in New York, how he felt, what he was working on now, when he'd come back to permanently live in the country.

Never, repeated Fred in his mind as he looked at his mother gathering cookie crumbs into a leaflet, the stuffed bear under her arm. He knew he'd abandon her again, this time forever. He had no chance. He would feel guilty unto death.

In the few days that he stayed in Bucharest, he didn't leave the house. No one sought him out, with the exception of a former colleague who had called to ask him if he could help his son, who was soon to go to a college in New York. He stayed up at night remembering moments and scenes from another life, the life that was no longer his. Mimi called to ask how the launch had gone and kept rattling on:

"Ah, Fred, I imagine it was a triumph! How many people were there? Hundreds? Did they break the library's windows, like in the old days? Did your hand cramp up from too many autographs? I suspect that you were besieged by TV reporters. A party at Athene Palace afterward? Ah, how I would have liked to have been there, too! And your mother caught everyone's eye, taking charge as always from the front row, proud of you! And possessive! The queen-mother! Greet her for me. Look, I can close my eyes and see it all! You must be so happy! I feel so bad that I wasn't there to savor the success and glory with you! Kisses, darling. I can't wait to hear about it from you. Good night! But what am I saying? It must be morning there. Good morning, darling!"

He'd fall asleep around dawn, sometimes fully clothed. He'd forget to brush his teeth, and he hadn't shaved since he'd arrived in Bucharest. He dreamt that he went into dirty water that rose up to his ankles, and he desperately flailed in the air, sensing that he'd drown. He dreamed of trees fallen to the ground. He heard the painful movement of a saw. Another night, he dreamed that mice went into his shoes, and he trembled helplessly. When you dream of mice, you'll lose something, Mimi had once told him, her mind on her stocks, which had fluctuated for some days. Nonsense, said his aunt. Mice mean the fear of something.

He looked into the mirror and almost got scared. He had grown whiter. New wrinkles were on his forehead; his cheeks were gaunt, his hair disheveled, his shoulders slumped. Mimi was right: he was getting smaller and smaller. His aunt gave him a bottle of Advil for the headache he continued to complain about.

"Take some *extraveral* too, it calms you down," she'd say whenever they met in the dark ivy-shaded apartment.

A ghost haunted the ghost-haunted home.

"I'll give you some of mine. How can you take it otherwise? We're all on *extraveral*. Even before freedom came upon us."

The same *Before*, an indefinite era invoked during good times and bad, the only reference point in day-to-day conversation that gave a meaning to the chaos of the transition. Or whatever that time was called that was neither communist anymore nor capitalist yet. A legislative anarchy controlled politically so as to give leeway to the birth of the new upper class, the great burglars that would legalize corruption, later perpetuated democratically.

His aunt watched him piteously, sometimes with angry bouts.

"Go and see about your life. Eva would have told you so. At least save yourself. And send us money. We might need to get another woman to help. I can't do everything by myself. God help us!"

Dinu took him to the airport and handed him two packages of books, his author's copies.

"Have a pleasant flight. And take care over Labrador!"

5

WITH EACH PASSING YEAR, THE PROFITS at *Mimosa I* and *II* beauty salons grew considerably. Mimi was now the president of a veritable beauty-empire. She traveled between New York and Nantucket, moved among influential circles, and the more tired she got from work and social events, the more she seemed to thrive. *Elle* magazine had dedicated a page to her. She also appeared in *Harper Bazar*: "The Adventure of an Emigrant from Ceaușescu's Dictatorship on Fifth Avenue." Mimi smiled intelligently in a photograph taken in her office, its windows facing Central Park.

She spoke simply and convincingly about how one can cheat time and fool death using methods hitherto unknown in the West, molded from clay, applying ancient formulas and mud packs from a miraculous lake.

"The body has to keep up with the soul," she decreed, citing the publicity slogan of the *Mimosa* salons. "The business of plastic surgery will go bankrupt," she foretold at the end of the article. "Prolonging your youth needn't be a traumatic process. Maintaining your beauty doesn't have to be a painful act as long as there exist secrets that activate our biological resources that are ignored by our civilization, which only gives credit to pills and scalpels."

But she had gotten silicon breasts and injected Botox. These didn't impede her from adopting the Pharisaical attitude of the American advertising industry. To pretend means more than to be. A world that exists in images and appearances. What could be more convincing?

"I'm the best publicity for my clinics. I'm the proof that we have natural resources to weaken time and make it our ally." She quoted here from Fred's old thinking. Only he had lost himself in the leaves of time. The article had an unexpected effect: the number of clientele went through the roof.

Fred was running in place, and Mimi perceived this as her only failure. She saw him as a locked iron bunker, whose key she could not find. She forced open doors behind which Fred had hidden his inability, and he slammed closed the ones that might have led, if not to a solution, at least to the illusion of salvation. He had returned from Romania even more blasé, spoke even less than before, left his home more rarely. They made love less often. Sometimes he heard his thoughts roar. He would close his eyes and see words that strode over each other, went into each other, onto an absurd and heavy canvas. He wrote with increasing difficulty, unmotivated and hopeless.

Mimi looked at him helplessly, sometimes unable to hide her fury though—much as his aunt had looked at him in Bucharest.

"Do something. Save yourself!" Mimi said to him one evening.

"Save myself from what? I'm not at sea. No storm threatens me. Quite the opposite. Nothing is happening."

"Exactly. You're wallowing in shallow waters."

"But you're on a wave, Mimi. Sometimes I see you as a huge, bright-blue ship passing over the horizon. My eyes can no longer follow you."

Mimi changed her tone:

"What should I do to help you get out of this mood?"

"There's nothing to be done."

Fred closed the book, lit his pipe and turned his back to her, looking out the window toward Central Park, where carriages pulled tourists slowly alongside cyclists and ambitious runners.

"Why don't you go out to walk a bit in the park?" she asked him, then glanced at her watch and jerked in fear. She threw her handbag over her shoulder, put on her dizzyingly high heels and cried from the hallway:

"God! I should have been at the Metropolitan Club already. There's a reception that I can't miss. All the press will be there. I need to run. Will you be all right?"

"Sure, Mimi, I'll get better and better. Leave in peace."

She didn't hear his last words as the door shut behind her. Fred's gaze was stuck on a pigeon that had perched a bit on the windowsill and shaken its neck.

When it saw his face behind the curtain, it flew away frightened, as if plunging itself into emptiness.

Mimi's business went splendidly until one evening her accountant troubled the waters when he called her saying he absolutely wanted to come over. He couldn't say anything on the phone, and he didn't want to postpone it until the following day.

"What could be so important? At this hour? At my home? This guy is getting out of control!"

Mimi was shocked. Soon after, the doorman called her intercom to let her know that she had a guest. There was the accountant at the door, confused and sweaty. He didn't greet anyone. He ignored Fred and whispered hastily to Mimi that they needed to talk alone.

The two retreated to the guest room as Fred went back to his office. Now and then he heard Mimi's yells. He couldn't understand what she said, but her voice carried a sometimes guttural and thin accent, as it did back when she couldn't control herself, when she didn't struggle to adopt the attitude of high-society women that didn't raise their voices and have inappropriate reactions, as though they'd just heard an announcement about the end of the world.

Fred lit his pipe. He felt his chest grow heavy and his temples throb as if he were in Bucharest and heard his mother's deep voice crying from the dining room: "Where have you all gone?"

Almost an hour later, Mimi went into the living room, threw her shoes off as she always did when some emotion overwhelmed her, and collapsed on the couch with her head in her hands. The accountant had left as mysteriously and sweaty as he had arrived, closing the door behind him. Mimi sat there, suspiciously quiet. Fred didn't leave his office for fear of an earthquake. He foresaw it. Mimi had taught him to listen to her senses, to pay attention to signs and premonitions, while he had lectured her on logic and reason.

The IRS had begun an investigation into the two *Mimosa* clinics. They were after her old business partner Adam Morgan, who was suspected of having conducted a Ponzi scheme of investments and fraudulent banking operations with various clients and organizations. He had secretly used stocks and bonds under her name. Morgan had been arrested and the scandal made its way to the press. Her accountant gave her another, even more awful piece of news: the two salons' profits hadn't been fully declared fully on her taxes.

Sheppard was nowhere to be found. After a long while, he sent her a message that he was vacationing on an island whose name he didn't want to divulge.

Nightmarish days and weeks followed. Mimi decided that she'd sleep in the guest room for a while. She needed peace and quiet, or rather a space where her restlessness could manifest itself unabated.

She would wake up very early, put on her large sunglasses to hide the dark circles around her eyes, and hastily leave the room. Fred treated her gently, tried to speak to her, to understand just how serious the situation was, to console her, to give her courage. Her tears and desperation alternating with her cries and wounded animal whimpers made him feel ill. He couldn't even concentrate on reading anymore.

He began to be afraid. It was a generalized unde-fined fear, which began with Mimi and extended itself to the water that flowed in the bathroom, to the sound of the microwave when she warmed her coffee, the ele-vator when it stopped with a thump on their floor, or the telephone which rang only to give more bad news. It was the fear of sounds, the fear of objects, the fear of torrential summer rain when the black sky descended on the windows.

Mimi was gone all day long, and at night she gave vent in bouts of fury. He awaited her in fear, not knowing what to expect every time she came into the house slam-ming the door, throwing her shoes in the middle of the room and hurrying to the fridge, where she took out all sorts of ice cream cartons that she devoured while con-tinuing to talk—even to herself, if Fred wasn't around.

"Tax evasion, do you understand? A crime!"

"What can happen?" he asked using a soft voice.

"They can arrest me, that's what can happen! Close up my salons, confiscate my accounts, take everything from us. We'll wind up under a bridge. Ah, how stupid! To fall into the trap of those insatiable monsters!"

"I warned you…."

"You have no idea what this is all about! You warned me… What did you want me to do? They're all dirty. I'll fire them all! Sheppard first of all! In the end, they made money off me, not I off them."

"Do you think it's wise to fire him now?"

"I don't know what's wise. You're the wise one, the mindful one, the mind-person. I'm just a leg-person, aren't I? I know how you think!"

"Don't get upset, Mimi. I was just thinking that it's not a good moment to turn them against you."

"Better against me than with me! I've paid them handsomely and look at the shit they've gotten me into. But don't worry: if something happens to me, they're going down with me. I won't give up so easily! I'll hire the best financial experts, accountants, lawyers. I'll spend everything, to the last penny. I made the money. I'll spend it all. *I* made the money not the other way around! Because we're only talking about money here. I was wrong to give interviews for those popular magazines. I exposed myself," cried Mimi as she scooped up more ice cream. "I attracted attention; I was first. Everything's about competition here. The law of the jungle. They went for my jugular!"

On other evenings she'd sit on the couch with her legs underneath her, crying her eyes out while Fred strolled around quietly stroking his beard and seeking words, feeling just as powerless as she was.

"I don't want to become poor again, Fred. I've broken my back working in this country."

One evening, after drinking more than usual, she made polenta as she wept and poured it into champagne glasses. Fred looked at her from his armchair through the opened door, how she talked to herself between hiccups and pulled on her hair.

"What will become of us? After achieving so many good things, you don't want to go back where you started. Look, this is what we'll have instead of Veuve Clicquot! Screw this polenta of a life!"

She brought home boxes full of documents, contracts from the salons, everything she could find and carry before the beginning of the investigation. The guest room where she had deposited them looked like a financial institution from the old days. Mimi roamed about feverishly, not knowing what she was looking for. Sometimes she fell asleep with her head on the files.

The news that Morgan had had a heart attack after his arrest and died several hours later at a hospital in Manhattan triggered an even bigger breakdown.

"Now that the big shark has kicked the bucket, they'll be coming after me. Be careful: they'll start to harass us. Don't open the door to anyone if I'm not home. They might come to search the house. And don't answer the phone, either. Wait until the voice message picks up. We'll be watched, recorded, photographed."

"Who would do this, Mimi?"

"What do you mean who? They have agents everywhere."

"That sounds like Big Brother. I'll reread Orwell."

"Well, what else can you do? You know that they kept me in an office for six hours a few days ago? They even asked me what I used to eat as a child."

Fred stared at her suspiciously. Her face didn't seem at all horrified, but he felt fear gnaw at his bones.

Sometimes the scenes escalated badly. She would throw everything off the table, break Sevres dishes and Baccarat glasses, cut her expensive dresses to shreds and mutilate shoe heels. Fred stared at her timidly, testing the waters.

"Stop blaming yourself so much. Blame is the most frightening of monsters. It can paralyze you."

"Look at yourself! You've been paralyzed for so long! And you're innocent! You're as clean as a tear, a tiny Jesus descended to Earth to give me lectures. Why didn't you put your soul and back into it then, to make money, to make it, since that's why we came over here, didn't we? For you to write your great masterpiece! I've given you all the comfort in the world, put you on a pedestal, carried everything on my back, and what did I get in the end? The IRS on my tail! Don't talk to me about guilt! The most frightening monster... I'm tired of your worthless philosophy. Eh, let's see how you'll live off it if something happens to me!"

Fred would run to his office and close the door behind him. Fear is stronger than humility, but how could he explain that to her?

"Where are you going? Come back!" cried Mimi. "You don't even have balls enough to face me! What a fate! I could have chosen a strong man to support me, someone like Sheppard; screw him too! He's disappeared like a scoundrel. Come back here!"

The hearings lasted until the fall. Mimi was not paralyzed at all and moved efficiently, as if she had fought all her life against extreme institutions and situations. She had hired a team of legal experts, answered all the solicitations, turned over all the documents that she was asked to, and the investigation was officially declared closed. The IRS left her alone after her Nantucket salon went bankrupt; she closed her business and paid about $1,000,000 in fines.

She returned to the bedroom and resumed sleeping well, along with her exercise and spiritual practice. She refreshed her wardrobe, threw all the sweets and ice cream out of the fridge and warned Fred with an authoritarian smile:

"Eh, we don't have the money we had before, but we'll survive. With more prudence and moderation..."

Fred also smiled, ironically. The last two words seemed aimed at him. He was the imprudent and extravagant one, in Mimi's words, who had wrought havoc all those years.

"I still have to get better. Starting tomorrow I'm going back to yoga and Pilates. My joints have gone stiff. And I'll have to meditate non-stop to catch up with my class. Do you think that objects can be moved just by looking at them?"

For Fred, nothing had ended. He twitched every time the phone rang. Sometimes it seemed to him that there were noises down the hall, in front of their apartment. He looked through the peephole and stood glued to the door, afraid until he didn't hear anything anymore. And even then he was suspicious: perhaps they, the IRS agents, had hidden on a staircase? Mimi had told him once that agents might search their home looking for documents and evidence. It hadn't happened, but Fred continued to panic.

Although Mimi had assured him that everything was normal, that they would have peace and quiet again, he couldn't escape the tension of the preceding months which had triggered moods in him that were difficult to control.

"We're starting a new stage, my dear: *Mimi's life, Episode Two. Or Season Two,*" she laughed while Fred tried to light his pipe. "Oh, even better: *Before and After the Fall.* What do you say?"

Fred stared at her quietly from his armchair facing the window.

"I'm asking you seriously. How about this title? *Before and After the Fall...* I love it! And it's so true!"

The same *Before* and *After* that he had heard in Romania, the same folds and cracks into which people and empires rise and fall.

One evening she came with something else:

"My dear, I'm thinking of writing a book. I'm serious. You should give me some tips..."

It was the first time she spoke to him in English. Fred smiled, though inside he writhed. Mimi seemed surer of herself than ever, and as she spoke that phrase with a perfect accent, he felt her even more distant, a free bird that flapped its wings over his head.

"Do you think it's a good idea? Don't you see what a torment writing is?" said Fred.

"Don't think about yourself. You don't really write; you contemplate writing. And the torment you speak of is the perfect excuse. I want to write a real, simple, honest book. For people."

Mimi said she wanted a book for people, not for birds, as he wrote them. Honest, and therefore not mystified by phantasmagoric thoughts. Plus, Mimi told him that she'd write directly in English.

"Mimi, you need to approach words with respect and fear. Just as you approach truth and the sky, the seas and oceans—with humility, acknowledging that they're not your habitat, protecting their mystery."

"Great advice! Exactly what I expected from you. Only that I'll approach them with passion and curiosity. That's healthier than fear and humility which are for losers, cowards and philosophers. We'll see…"

Mimi's schedule became busy again. She was gone in the evenings off to receptions and worldly happenings, as Fred's migraines and fears grew worse. He seemed paranoid for nothing. Once, he complained that the maid went through the drawers. Maybe she was looking for something compromising; maybe she was even an agent of the IRS that had infiltrated their home. Another time he alleged that he had been photographed in the street and followed all the way to his home by a dubious man. What if they, the IRS officers were still after her? What if they were still keeping an eye on them?

"Fred, I told you that the case is closed. I was completely cleared. Enough! What's with your paranoia? Have you gone insane?"

The words which he had heard long ago or read somewhere resounded in his ears: never speak to a madman about madness. He twitched, squeezed his fingers into fists and felt his temples explode.

"Go somewhere for a while. Leave the city. Why not spend some days in Florida? My parents would love to see you."

"No way."

"Or go to Romania to see your mother. Stay with her, take care of her for a little while."

"I don't want to go anywhere, Mimi. You can't run from fears—or from yourself."

"Then spare me your breakdowns! Go to a therapist!"

He went. He sat down on the couch and was quiet for 50 minutes during the first session. The therapist pretended to listen to his silence, to hear his thoughts, and suggested to him that next time he should read something from the book he was supposedly writing. That didn't work either.

Fred stretched on the couch and deepened his silence, but the well-paid minutes in which the psychiatrist guarded his silence did him well. As a concession, or to repay his patience, or just from politeness, he finally agreed to write some imaginary letters to read to him in the therapy sessions.

Fear, Mimi, fear. The most perverse beast to come from Pandora's box. The one that sets limits, swells helplessness like a carbuncle ready to erupt, emanating nasty-smelling liquids. What expression is this: "To live with fear in your chest?" How would you live with a mouse moving around under your shirt? Or a claw clenching your heart? I have always lived with fear in my chest, Mimi. I have felt its claws shredding my skin. I have felt its cold breath, the smell of a foreign body transplanted under my shirt, pierced through my stomach. Fear is organic, a physical phantom, ugly, twisted, with teeth and hair that grin at you from every corner, every mirror you might look into. It's there, on the prowl. Like death. I know you don't care about my fear of the future, of the past, my fear in front of a white sheet of paper or in front your appealing legs, my fear of the ring of the phone at night or the dripping of water in the sink, impossible to stop; the fear of being rejected, or leaving or staying where I am, as I am.

I've been fearful since I can remember. Long trains of phantoms have visited me at various ages. The darkness, beneath the cloak of a decapitated soldier during the nights after which the news came to me that Father had perished on the front, far from home, for a now inexplicable cause, when utopias took on the inhuman face of a crippled history.

Loneliness in adolescence, when I ejaculated humili-atingly under my plaid blanket, which I received as a gift from a lively aunt with thick-rimmed glasses who smoked contraband cigars, read foreign books and wore transpar-ent skirts and nylon shirts glued to her sweltering breasts.

Uncertainty and doubt. When I finished writing a book and lay for weeks afterward with my mind squeezed dry and my soul emptied, on the brink of depression and exhaustion, asking myself, what's it all worth? Where are my words going, my years; how much longer can delusion keep me warm when the cold wind blows through all the rooms of my being?

The culprit, a veiled phantom that appeared on the threshold of new life-segments or crossroads, admonishing me with a carbonized finger pointing toward the sky that I didn't take the road I should have taken, hadn't made the right choice, and that the path I had chosen would lose itself in forests or be swallowed by water.

The fear in the dream, more tangible than all lived fears, that I'm running after my own shadow and when I reach it, it disappears swallowed by sand, and I awake naked, sometimes bodiless, other times without a voice. My legs sink in the soil. I can't yell or run. The fear that some morning I'll wake up as somebody else, in another room, without memories, without you, as I was scared in my childhood that Mother would abandon me, forget me in a park or store. Later, she confessed that she had lived with the same fear of me disappearing, of losing me. In the end, I abandoned her. She died alone, far away, just *as she appeared in my dream, a bird that no longer had the strength to fly and froze on the threshold of a house in mid-winter.*

He didn't go to Bucharest that winter. He couldn't go. He had returned with a bitter taste after the launch of his novel. He had left his mother somewhat stable, cutting out strips with his name from newspapers.

"The fragile heart has stumbled," his aunt said on the phone. "Maybe she waited for you so she could die having made her peace. Maybe the reunion was too much for her."

These words increased his guilt. The guilt that he had waited so many years to return. The guilt that had come back when he exposed his mother to deep emotions by introducing her to everyone at the bookstore, just after she might have found her balance. She was timid, like him. Too sensitive. She had learned to live alone. His visit ruined her equilibrium, reopened wounds, forcing her back to a past where all the doors had been slammed shut and locked tight.

The phone rang very early in the morning. Mimi had just gone out to swim—as she started every day—in the pool on the top floor. He jumped from his bed with fear in his chest.

"She died suddenly, no pain. Cardiac arrest. You don't need to come. Good thing you got to spend some time with her; she saw you, touched you. Now, anyway, it doesn't matter. I'm taking care of everything. It'll be all right. Send money. I'll send you pictures from the funeral," his aunt added.

He went back to bed with his feet icy, as in his childhood when he felt some big emotion: before an exam, a girl he loved in secret, or some uncovered lie. His cheeks would grow red and his legs would immediately freeze. He lay numb, staring at the ceiling until Mimi returned, full of energy, ready to take on the world no matter what it had to offer. From beneath the blanket pulled up to his chin, Fred whispered brazenly:

"Mother died."

"What are you saying?" cried Mimi, half of her in the closet where her dresses were neatly arranged according to color.

"Mother died."

The voice lowered into his body.

"Speak louder, I can't hear you!"

He turned his face to the wall. No one could hear him. But what if he'd become entirely mute, as he sometimes dreamed? What if he'd passed into the great silence? He had gone through such an episode in his adolescence. He didn't know what had come over him, whether it was from the lectures, the existentialists, the dreams, the surrealists, or some unrequited love, or perhaps merely the revolt of hormones seeking to defy the absurd.

Back then, he'd suddenly made up his mind that he didn't wish to speak anymore. He felt good in the quiet world of moving forms. He spoke only in his thoughts.

It was the age at which his voice molted, and he didn't like to hear himself. His mother had respected his choice, pretended to understand him, and asked him to write to her whatever he refused to say. Something happened then. At first he wrote simple phrases. Later, he filled up entire pages. His mother read them attentively, never mocking him. The fiction that would take over grew in him.

"That's how I became a writer," Fred would relate to his audience at readings. "Facing the silence. Squeezing out the words that deserved to make themselves heard. And in this silence my imagination flowered. Back then, I had peace and time, which I no longer have."

He received photographs from the chapel, from the cemetery and from the lunch that followed, a bunch of receipts with what had been spent, and a tiny card on which his aunt had written only:

"It was good. I paid a lawyer to take care of the inheritance and whatever else needs taking care of. I hope you don't have any claims to the apartment. People say you hit the jackpot in America. It would be nice if you left the apartment to my son. After all, he's your only nephew."

He left it to him. He would never return to Bucharest. On the night his mother died his insomnia returned, and it would stick with him till the end.

6.

THE THERAPIST WAS A MIDDLE-AGED MAN
with such a melancholic glance and such a soft voice that
he seemed sad. Fred had never seen him smile, in any
case. Each time, Fred would lie down on the couch and
be silent for several minutes. His throat would slowly
loosen and his Adam's apple would claim its place again
after several unsuccessful attempts to jump out.

They were both silent, which by itself might have been
good therapy to quiet the noise of Fred's thoughts. The
thundering of hooves stopped, and the therapist waited
patiently, listening until a calm air came over Fred's mind.
The therapist always began with the same exclamation:

"So, then!", which played the role of untying the
discussion from where they had left off the last session or provoking Fred to voice aloud the thoughts
that were running through his mind at that moment.

After several sessions in which Fred's imaginary letters, always addressed to Mimi, came to a standstill,
the therapist asked him to keep a diary, to describe his
sensations and dreams.

"You don't ask that of a writer," Fred defended himself in fear of the white sheet of paper, a slope on which
he had slipped intensely and easily once, and on which

he now stood frozen, incapable of any movement, dizzied by the path that things might have taken had he finally let go. "I kept apart from dream-like literature in Romania when it was all the rage, and maybe then it might have served me in camouflaging the truth about a failed system, in veiling the political aspects; the censors always looked over my shoulder at what I wrote, but now I'm not interested in keeping a dream-notebook. I think this has to do with age," Fred excused himself. "What's more, it's always seemed to me that keeping a journal and writing down your dreams are forms of narcissism. They seem artificial in some way, if not exhibitionist—naïve pretexts of stroking your vanity while claiming complexity."

The therapist didn't seem to care, or didn't want to care. He only recorded Fred's fear of getting close to himself, even in a roundabout way.

"And I don't even know where the dream ends, actually. I don't dream of my mother, for example; I see her."

"But how do you know it's her?"

"I simply know."

In one of the sessions Fred gave his blue notebook to the therapist as a concession he made to him, or as a sign of sympathy for his discretion in not forcing him into any uncomfortable terrain.

I can recognize her among a thousand birds. As soon as I am alone somewhere, she comes and settles down close to me, by my side. I always see her sideways—thin, with a long, outstretched, elegant neck, just as she was, frail but powerful. Sometimes she has black feathers with shades of bright blue; other times her chest is orange and her tiny beak is red, like a wild rose hip. She sits still and stares at me with her right eye, fearful and ready to take flight at my slightest gesture. I have learned that she wants me neither to speak nor to get closer to her. Maybe she's not allowed to do more, I think. It's already extraordinary that she is allowed to come. I feel the moment she appears with excitement. It happens when I'm alone, when I'm afraid, in my moments of panic but also when it seems to me that I could change everything around, that equilibrium is just as relative as confusion, that I still have the strength to stop the snowball that has been rolling down a hill getting bigger and bigger, squashing me despite my struggles, for quite a long time. Sometimes I'm clear-headed. I feel my blood run through my veins. My muscles throb with the strength of youth. I am here, now, self-confident, a perfect representation of the fine line between the temptation to continue and more seductive abandonment. Then I become unsure, hesitant, stopped in mid-air like a wounded tree transplanted into foreign soil all too late.

"Go out, walk, do something," Mimi would sometimes explode.

Following the therapist's advice about how he should act with him during his periods of depression, Mimi gave up on talking quietly, calmly and slowly, as with a child who doesn't understand well or a sick person who must be shielded from the real intensities of a world from which he is isolated. But her normal voice became irritated when she saw how he sat in semi-obscurity crouched over a book, stroking his beard with a heavy and melancholic look, apparently serene. Just like his mother. Her affection weakened, her compassion turned to frustration. What was she guilty of? What more could she do? The defeated ones become insufferable.

"You stay in the house all day and split hairs. You've made a hole in that armchair. And give up those somber books; can't you see that they're no help? Instead of choosing something that might save you, you keep on looking for dark stories."

"Books aren't life vests, Mimi. You can sink with them. I keep on thinking it's actually culture that estranges you. It gives you a thread; you become excited, believing that you can climb to where the thread seems to descend from, and in the end culture wraps itself around your neck and strangles you."

"Why don't you put this in your books?"

"It doesn't matter *what* you say as much as *how* you say it. And especially *when* you say it. Books are time. Everything is time in this world, an eternally flowing river. It takes you with it if you let go, from nowhere to nowhere. But this is the law, and it's good to submit to it. I wanted to come ashore sometimes. Other times I retreated only to contemplate its flow. I tried to go upstream, but hadn't accurately assessed water's strength. I think I started sliding backward when I lost hold of my conspiracy with time."

Mimi hesitated. She wasn't sure whether he was fooling around or was trying to give her an inferiority complex with his discourse, as in the old days, when she listened fascinated, convinced that fate had loved her by giving her a superior, intelligent and talented man. Now his words sounded empty, like balls thrown at walls. Mimi had neither patience nor curiosity left; life had flowed tumultuously for her, but without all these flights of fancy which obviously went nowhere and helped with nothing. Except to lose one's mind.

"You're the last person who should talk about time. You had all the time in the world," she answered sharply, bringing his thoughts back to the room that had suddenly become too tiny for the two of them.

"Don't get upset," said Fred in an attempt to prevent another of her crises.

"How can I not get upset? What? Do you think that time only passes for you? Look at the wrinkles I have by the corners of my eyes. And my neck. See!"

Mimi ripped off her shirt, expanding her chest and pushing her chin out.

"When have you last seen my neck? Not to mention other things…"

"You're very beautiful, Mimi. Calm down. I like you even like this. I mean as you are. Old age has its nobility."

"Old age?" cried Mimi.

"Understand words in their essence. What's old age, after all? The triumph of forms in a fragile shell. The age of quiet and inner peace."

"Are you stupid? What inner peace? My IRS nightmare has just ended. What peace with you stuffing that chair like a shriveled up vegetable? I hope that damn chair will crack one day and you'll crash with it into hell!"

"A beautiful image, Mimi. Can I steal it from you?"

"Steal it, fuck it, do what you want with it! Nothing will come of these ideas with which you've always boggled my mind. Where are your great books? Where? I sacrificed myself for you. For you to write, to have quiet, comfort, money, time."

Fred ran to the bathroom and locked the door behind him.

"Where are you running to? Come out!" yelled Mimi, until her vocal cords let out a sound that frightened even her. "You're a coward, that's what you are. You could never stand confrontation. Come back! I want us to talk, to talk!" Mimi shrieked uncontrollably. "Look what you've brought me to! Look what you've done to me! Come the hell out of there before I break the door!"

In the weeks that followed, his headaches grew worse, as did his fears. The psychiatrist increased his dosage of antidepressants and added some others pills. The therapist changed his method, but Mimi, overwhelmed by remorse, spent less time at home and tried to speak to him more calmly and more slowly.

Seby showed up then. He called, saying he'd lost track of Fred; asked him why he disappeared and said that he wanted to come over. He showed up radiantly, younger and taller than before, with a bottle of Irish whiskey. After looking at all the paintings in the living room, he sat down on the couch and said in a self-satisfied way:

"In the end, your manuscript fell into the best hands. My literary agent, without a doubt the best right now, has agreed to represent you. She liked your book, and next Monday she'll call you to go and sign the contract. Of course, no one can guarantee anything, but she has a nose for what she does and she's rarely wrong. It's a big agency, the biggest. They've represented Kundera, Llosa, Saramago. She told me that she already has some publishers in mind to send the book to. Of course, you'll have to agree to their suggestions then, you might have to cut here and there, change what needs to be changed. You know how it is: your editor, your master!"

Fred had heard this in Romania too, in the old days, when political censors would suggest a cut here or there. Back then he was ready to fight for every paragraph, having made up his mind not to make any concessions despite not being published. He might have accepted the marketplace's censorship in the U.S., but the big news he had long awaited came too late. He had no reaction.

"My dear, let's drink, then. Welcome to America! I wish I could have done this sooner, but maybe it wasn't the right time... Remember, they said the same to us during communism: *It's not the right time, comrades!*"

Seby laughed, filled the glasses that Fred had placed on the table in front of the couch and only then seemed to look at him carefully. Fred's hands trembled; he had dark circles under his eyes and a blank look.

"But how are you? Do you feel well?" asked Seby sipping his whiskey.

After Seby left, Fred stayed in the darkness with his pipe between his stiff fingers. Mimi was late. He didn't know what the time was; he no longer kept track of the time. He heard the elevator and jumped up all of a sudden. The noise startled him. Perhaps the secret agents had heard about his book and were now coming to search the apartment? The novel criticized both systems plentifully. It criticized life under communism, but also the walls found in the free world. If they came to take him, he'd get pulled through tribunals, humiliated, terrorized. He felt lost without Mimi.

When she wasn't home, the horror spread through every room. He saw eyes in the curtains and shadows trickling down the walls. Hurriedly, he made his way to the window and drew the heavy curtains. He didn't dare go out in the hallway and opened the closet and hid himself there shaking, his ears pricked. Soon afterward, the voices of women could be heard. He remained in the closet, trying to figure out who it was. He heard Mimi looking for him. But who were the others? What if this was a trap? He stayed in his hiding place until Mimi came into the room and saw his shoes caught between the closet door.

"Fred! What are you doing there? Come out! What's wrong with you? Have you completely lost your mind?"

He came out slowly, like a child caught in the act, sweating, still trembling.

"I was afraid."

"Afraid of what, for God's sake?"

"I don't know. I heard voices."

"I came home with Jessica and Helen. Jessica will fix us something to eat, and then she'll work on bills for the salon."

"Bills? Did something happen?"

"Nothing happened, Fred. Relax, all's well. We have a large order of creams and antioxidants. Everything's going smoothly, better than before. Stop being so worried. How many times do I have to tell you? Come meet Helen, my *ghost writer.*"

"Goat?"

"Ghost!"

"A phantom?"

"Right! She's my phantom," whispered Mimi. "I'll dictate the book to her, and she'll write it under my name. That's how it's done here, Fred. You get a professional; can't go wrong that way. Helen wrote several successful books for big stars. Of course, her name doesn't show up. She doesn't exist. Do you understand? *She's a ghost!* We're starting tonight. A chapter per day. In a month the book will be done."

"You can't do this, Mimi. It's fraud, yet again! It's shameful."

"What's shameful is to hide in the closet and not come out and say *good evening* to these enchanting ladies," shouted Mimi over her shoulder.

She took out her scarf, threw off her shoes and opened a champagne bottle, then sat down on the couch satisfied.

Jessica clanked dishes in the kitchen, then brought in trays with cheese and fruits. Helen took out her recorder, opened her laptop and sat on the armchair by Mimi's feet.

Fred stared at them through the door opening. A picture worthy of Scheherazade. Only that his vision blurred and his knees softened all of a sudden. He lay numb on the bed as he heard the voices crisscrossing in the other room. He saw dark shadows rushed from his forehead, dancing grotesquely by him, making waves, distorted forms like ghosts of smoke. His heart was racing, the air had thinned, the walls closed in. He experienced a feeling of weightlessness and suffocation. That's how he'd later describe it to the therapist. Anxiety associated with severe depression would be the psychiatrist's diagnosis.

He was prescribed other pills that caused other side effects. The monster of depression crushed his body like a liana that feeds off of a once-healthy organism to fulfill its devastating destiny.

"What's Fred doing? Isn't he coming to have a glass of champagne with us?" asked Jessica. "I haven't seen him for some time."

"I think he fell asleep," Mimi made an excuse for him drily. "He's had a hard day."

7.

A MONTH LATER, MIMI FINISHED DICTATING her book and an Indian summer hit New York, a friendly autumn with honey-light, a reprieve before the incidental rains and the stifling cold that would come. The leaves on the trees had begun to change colors in Central Park.

Fred now stayed in bed late. Sometimes he spent his entire day in his pajamas. He had lost weight and quit smoking his pipe. His sole pleasure was watching the pigeons that sometimes landed on the windowsill. He didn't feed them. He looked at their agitated movements, the way in which they twisted their heads so suddenly, how they twitched nervously only to then take flight among the skyscrapers. If only to be a bird. To float freely. Like his mother.

It was just another weekday, and yet it was perfect. A clear morning with clean thin air that lessened the sound and agitation of the city. You could almost hear the fluttering of birds' wings on the upper stories of the buildings that surrounded Central Park. It was one of those mornings where people feel lighter, full of zest for life, their morale heightened.

"Your biorhythm is awful, Fred," repeated Mimi. "Get yourself out of this phase. Fight a bit! Find something to do. How about seeing your friends?"

Fred had stopped answering her for quite a while. He hadn't touched her in months. They shared the apartment; otherwise, each saw about his own life: Mimi, tumultuous, on the outside; Fred, anxious and mawkish within.

"This is no life!" lamented Mimi, oscillating between pity and fury.

What friends? Fred thought. Sam had died. Jim had left for two years in Bali. As for Seby, no way; he couldn't have ruined Seby's mood with a drowned man like himself. Mimi knew it, too. She preferred to stay out more than at home, tired of seeing him somber, crouched on the bed in a fetal position. He was only a shadow of the man she had once admired unto veneration. Yes, she had been his creation, she had allowed herself to be patronized by his elevated spirit. She had read the books he placed in her hands, had hung on his every word. But up to a point. When his eyes began to grow empty, his muscles began to lose their vigor, and he groped about confusedly among once-brilliant ideas, which had become enclosures he had once owned and among which he was no longer at home. Their boat crashed ashore. Mimi finally got out of the cage and flew away.

On that October morning, Mimi went into his room, pulled back the curtains and opened the window.

"Come on, Fred. Get up! It's a perfect day! Keep the window open to let the sun in. Come on, enough! Up! You haven't showered for days and look how your beard has grown!"

He obeyed. Her voice sounded like his mother's. He got out of bed slowly, covered his eyes to shield himself from the sunlight, lay still for a while staring at his bare feet on the carpet, looked at Mimi embarrassedly and said automatically:

"A perfect day."

"Pay attention. Follow me, please. Take your pills and put on your clothes properly. This afternoon a team of reporters will come to interview me and take some pictures for the book cover."

"What book?"

"Come on, Fred. Don't mess with me! I've told you a hundred times. My autobiography, remember? The one with the recommendations for beauty and rejuvenation treatments. The one I wrote with Helen…"

"What about her?"

"Oh, Lord, you drive me nuts! I've signed the contract. It'll be published in a few weeks. Don't you remember that I told you that they gave me a $100,000 advance? I promise you that after the book tour we'll go to Paris. A present for our anniversary."

"An advance of $100,000?"

"Yes, Fred, successful books bring lots of money here. My publisher guarantees that it'll be a best-seller.

I won't say any more… But you could have… too… You understand me."

"Beauty and rejuvenation treatments?"

"Stop repeating after me. Come on, go and change your clothes. And don't forget to take your medicine, please. Maybe double the dose today, to make sure nothing will happen like when… You know what I'm talking about. I'm going to run now to the hair salon and then I'll buy some flowers and come home to wait for the reporters. If you don't mind, I'd like to use your chair and this desk when I give my interview. You know, it looks better with books in the background. A bit of intellectual atmosphere counts for something."

Fred no longer heard her. Mimi left quietly locking the door after her. Fred went to the bathroom, washed himself for a long time, trimmed his beard with care, put on a blue striped shirt—Mimi's favorite—and swallowed his pills. A pleasant breeze blew from outside, and Fred felt good for the first time after weeks of agony. He even cleaned his desk and picked up some books from the bookshelves. He stared at their covers with care, but didn't dare open any of them. He could no longer concentrate to read, and he saw no meaning in it.

Suddenly, he heard the key turning in the front door and listened closely. It couldn't be Mimi; too soon, she left a few minutes ago; besides, he always recognized her by the noise she made, jingling the keys, stomping on the marble with her thin heels. No sound.

A cold shiver went down his spine. Had the IRS agents come to take him? At the same moment, the phone began to ring. A grave and strange sound, like a ship's siren. Mimi had told him for a long time not to answer the phone, to listen to the voice message. The agents harassed them non-stop.

The maid came in the living room with a duster in one hand and a vacuum in the other.

"Mrs. Mimi sent me to clean your office."

He didn't believe her. Mimi hadn't warned him. This was surely a trick to meddle with his papers. He was convinced that she was the one who had stolen his manuscript, too.

"If you don't mind, could you go into the living room? Or maybe you'd do better out on the balcony until I finish? It's so lovely outside. A bit of fresh air would do you good."

Did she think he was mad? How could he go on the balcony? She'd lock him out there. He was lost without Mimi. And the vacuum looked like a little bomb. Maybe this is what the maid was planning, to blow up the entire apartment. His face was glazed with sweat, and his dizziness came back.

The phone rang again. This time he heard a thin hysterical sound. He waited for the message, paralyzed. It was Mimi; he could hardly recognize her voice, from fear. She told him that the maid would come to make the bed and clean the room where the interview and photography session would then take place.

He remained by the door, breathing heavily. He followed the woman's every move with great care, supervised her when she made the bed, afraid that she'd hide something or other of his under the pillow or mattress. When she was done, he led her to the door and locked it twice afterward. He was already exhausted. His temples felt as if they were bursting; his shirt was soaked with sweat.

He took another dose of pills and lay in his armchair. Everything is dangerous. You can't trust anyone or anything. Everyone betrays you. People and objects. Even the armchair betrayed him. And Jim. But as for Mimi, he didn't dare say anything. She might punish him. His head roared. He heard the doorbell ring. He jumped, downright shaking. Yes, the cleaning woman had given away the evidence pilfered from his room and they were coming now to arrest him. The long sound of the doorbell repeated. He crawled to the door with his last remaining strength. Voices could be heard, and the high walls of the corridor amplified their echoes. He looked through the peephole and nearly passed out.

A commando was behind the door. Armed men, long black boxes, doubtless pistols and guns. Floodlights to catch him no matter what corner he went into, microphones and handcuffs, an entire arsenal against him. It was obvious he had no way to escape. The doorbell could be heard again, followed by strong thumps on the door. Fred's body tensed. He opened the window, rushed forward and flew.

The noises in the hallway died down. The intercom rang to let the resident know that the shooting crew was at the door. The home phone also rang. Mimi's voice was happy and authoritative on the voice message:

"Fred, the reporters and photographers might get there before me. Open the door for them and be nice, please. I'm on my way home; bringing two dozens of yellow roses. You'll like them. Young and fresh, they seem to last forever."

Fred's body lay like a shadow stretched on the blacktop in front of the apartment building. A black bird had perched itself by his feet. It stared at him sideways, as birds stare at the world.